The Creator's Craft

The Creator's Craft

Existence: A Critique

JIM MELKO

RESOURCE *Publications* • Eugene, Oregon

THE CREATOR'S CRAFT
Existence: A Critique

Resource Publications
An Imprint of Wipf and Stock Publishers
199 W. 8th Ave., Suite 3
Eugene, OR 97401

www.wipfandstock.com

PAPERBACK ISBN: 978-1-5326-7855-4
HARDCOVER ISBN: 978-1-5326-7856-1
EBOOK ISBN: 978-1-5326-7857-8

12/02/25

Scripture quotations taken from The Holy Bible, New International Version®, NIV®. Copyright © 1973, 1978, 1984, 2011 by Biblica, Inc. Used with permission of Zondervan. All rights reserved worldwide. www.zondervan.com

Double-slit experiment image and modified images in Chapter 10 are from Wikimedia Commons contributors, "File:Double-slit.svg," Wikimedia Commons, https://commons.wikimedia.org/w/index.php?title=File:Double-slit.svg&oldid=1003322333 (accessed October 16, 2025)

To all those who listened to my developing ideas and read
through the early and current versions:

My wife, Deborah Melko
My daughter, Erica Melko
My son, Michael Melko
My mother, Mary Melko
My sister, Mary Burgner
My son-in-law, Luke Davis
My friend, Vaughn Welches
His friend, Dan Jones
My friend, Jim Chalker
My friend and colleague, Carlene Blake

Without them, this book would not have been possible.

Give me a place to stand and a lever long enough
and I will move the world.
—ARCHIMEDES

If there is no boundary to space-time, there is no need to
specify the behavior at the boundary—no need to know the
initial state of the universe. There is no edge of space-time at
which we would have to appeal to God or some new law to set
the boundary conditions for space-time. We could say, "The
boundary condition of the universe is that it has no boundary." The universe would be completely self-contained and not
affected by anything outside itself. It would neither be created
nor destroyed. It would just BE. As long as we believed the
universe had a beginning, the role of the creator seemed clear.
But if the universe is really completely self-contained, having no
boundary or edge, having neither beginning nor end, then the
answer is not so obvious: what is the role of a creator?
—STEPHEN HAWKING WITH LEONARD MLODINOW,
A BRIEFER HISTORY OF TIME

Why is there something rather than nothing?
—GOTTFRIED LEIBNIZ, "PRINCIPLES OF NATURE
AND GRACE BASED ON REASON"

Our facts are God's fiction.
—FROM THE ABANDONED ORIGINAL DRAFT OF
THE CREATOR'S CRAFT

Contents

Preface

ART IS ALWAYS BORN within a context greater than itself. The artist may paint a landscape, sculpt a statue, or write an epic novel—but ultimately, art is a limited impression of the reality in which its artist stands, succeeding when it leads its audience to a new perception of some facet of their existence.

Few would dispute that our Creator is an artist. However, when we discuss his context, we usually refer to heaven—but God created heaven. Personally, I doubt that our Creator is contained within a limitation of his own making.

No, God is outside our dimensions, and his context is eternity—but eternity is a real context with properties.

First and foremost of those properties, eternity is outside of time. It is not subject to Einstein's relativistic universe, nor to the quantum universe, nor even to existence itself. Yet it appears to have properties such as sequence—as in numerical sequences or sequences of order. Like it or not, the character of God as portrayed in the Bible's Old Testament *develops* in his relationship to man. He appears to be changed by his experiences.

Yet he testifies that he is I Am—unchanging, at least in terms of how he portrays himself to us. If he knows everything—the beginning and the end, the past and the future, what has been and what will be—then we may conclude that while he gains in experience, that experience is nevertheless a part of him throughout eternity. It therefore makes sense that if God's character develops, then he can identify a state of inexperience as distinct, or separate, from a state of experience—even though, since time is irrelevant, his ultimate state of experience is, was, and always will be within his reference.

In other words, one physical principle of God's context is sequence. Think of it as layers, like a transparent onion but with an infinite core. Sequence does not have to be related to time at all; it can simply chronicle the growth, or expansion, of experience. At x layer, experience a does not exist; at y layer, experience a does exist. Yet in its transparency, all layers are visible both from within and without.

An eternal entity would probably hunger for the expansion, for the growth of those layers. He would desire it. And God desires the experience of our love.

The implications of this desire are tremendous, and I am ill-equipped to describe them or elaborate on them. Rather, I choose to look at God as the Artist desiring to create.

In trying to portray the Artist's reality—that necessary context greater than our own—I am forced to impose the limitations of narration upon that context, and to grapple with my own restricted imagination. I am the painting trying to portray the multi-dimensional (or non-dimensional) artist from a two-dimensional canvas.

I therefore give myself license to use what I know to paint that canvas. If there is art, then there is focus and contrast and development and meaning. If there is an artistic work, there is an intended audience.

And where there is an artist, there must be a critic.

It amuses me to imagine that last point to be an eternal truth, however hellish it may seem.

Premise

GOD CREATED EVERYTHING THROUGH a process that connects us scientifically to his presence and perspective.

I

The Studio and the Critic

ALL AT ONCE, I found myself.

I suppose I could say I awoke, or that I realized I was in a room, but neither of those is quite right. I was suddenly in a place where I was aware of myself—not that I had been asleep or that I had been anywhere before—rather, that I had been everywhere I had ever been and now I was here.

To say I was in a room would not be quite right, either. It was a space that seemed contained in some way, with soft, indiscernible boundaries as if there were walls that couldn't quite decide to be walls, a floor and a ceiling that simply didn't want to be there.

There were two other presences in the room with me. First, and most commanding of my attention, was a cloud. This, too, defied description. No matter where I looked at it, my gaze slid off to the side—the visual equivalent of trying to pick up a drop of mercury. Overall, the cloud was gray, but it was threaded with iridescent colors that flashed brilliantly in hues far beyond any I had ever seen before. The cloud lacked shape because its edges did not quite exist; it was as if it were growing imperceptibly and yet too quickly to be observed.

It was also without apparent size, since there was nothing else with which to compare it. I had the sense that it was vast, that I was infinitesimally tiny beside it, yet I could sense that it too was much smaller than the room that confined us.

When I looked behind me, there was a man sitting on a canvas chair. He was such a normal-looking sight that he was actually shocking in such an odd circumstance. He was a bit small for the chair and he sat with one leg drawn up, hands clasped around the knee. He was dressed in walking shoes, jeans and a red-and-green flannel shirt. He seemed middle-aged, with black hair swept through with white, and a white goatee. His eyes were a bright blue, and they sparkled along with his smile as he regarded me.

"Hello?" I said with a start.

He nodded once and replied, "Welcome!"

I took a step back, then asked the obvious. "Where am I?"

He released his knee and slid off the chair to stand before me. "You are in the Artist's studio."

This did not help me at all, except that it explained the chair a little—the kind a director of a movie or a graphic artist would stereotypically use. Still, I felt as if he expected me to understand him, so I felt a bit stupid as I asked, "What artist?" Then I realized the answer. "Are you the artist?"

He laughed and clapped his hands together once. "Oh, no, no! I could never claim that honor! No, I am simply the critic."

Okay, so now I knew I was in an artist's studio with a critic.

This was not helpful.

I started over. "Where am I? Who are you?" If that sounded thick, I didn't care. I was completely confused.

He regarded me cheerfully for a moment in silence and then asked me the same question. "Tell me, who are you?"

The question, however, was suddenly the answer. Who am I? I am Jim Melko of southwest Ohio, and . . .

. . . and I am a baby in the bright lights of a hospital room, a child bundled in a stroller in the crisp outdoors, a boy in a cape leaping the neighbor's bushes, a teen driving to Oxford to visit my girlfriend, a young man taking her hand in a church, a professional accepting an administrative position at another university, a father of a newly born daughter, and then a newly born son, an agnostic accepting Christianity, a songwriter teaching others how to write songs, a teacher in an urban high school, a retiree, and even . . . an elderly man fighting health problems and reaching up from bed to turn out the light one last night.

I was all of these and more. I was all of the moments of my life's awareness, and I could sense the shadowy possibilities of choices I did not make and directions I did not take. None of these moments seemed closer to me nor more distant; I could not select any of them and say, "Here is where I left off." My birth was as immediate as my death, as was everything in between. I was more myself than I had ever been in any moment.

I took all of this in without a struggle—it was simply as it was and had been.

But all of it was in distinct contrast to now.

I faced the man, but I did not have to say anything to him. He simply looked at me and nodded, saying, "I see. And who am I?"

He sighed, then reached behind him and lifted himself back up into the chair. With a smile, he made a little motion with his hand, and I looked behind me to see another chair just like the first, only more my size. "Please, have a seat. I will explain."

As I sat, he looked over at the cloud and repeated, "I am the critic. This is the studio of the Artist, and that cloud there is his masterpiece—and your home. You are part of his work, and you are sitting here now because you wrote a book about all of this."

At this, I gave a start, because everything instantly made a certain amount of sense. Yes, I had written a book about all of this—the critic, the Artist, and the cloud—and I had to consider for a moment the idea that I was hallucinating: how could I be experiencing my own book? Yet even as that idea flashed through my mind, I knew it was wrong. I knew it completely—I could sense everything completely—I was totally *here*, and I could not doubt that. Yet I could not recall any of the details of my book beyond the current point.

"So you are the critic I wrote about. And this"—I gestured toward the cloud—"is existence. And the Artist is the Creator—God himself." Then I stopped. "But wait, that's not right." I turned to him. "You're not right. The critic isn't real. He's just something I made up, a literary device."

The critic spread his arms and looked down at himself. "Ah, but here I am!" He dropped his hands on his lap and looked at me with amusement. "You asked the reader to accept the idea of a critic for the purpose of your narrative, but now you say I shouldn't be here?"

I sat there, confused. He chuckled and said, "You needed me, so you made me up. Maybe you got it right. Or maybe I'm just a useful construct." He shrugged, lifting his palms up. "What difference does it make? But still, let's consider your logic.

"The Artist is an artist. As such, he needs an audience. The individual members of that audience will each bring their perspective to the work of an artist. As a critic, my role is to place each artist's work in context, in relation to both their previous work and the work of other artists, and to serve as a guide for the artist's audience to appreciate the full quality of the work. When necessary, I also point out the flaws, both to encourage stronger work from the artist and to highlight how it compares to other artistic work."

He paused for a moment, peering at me to gauge my understanding.

"But you're human," I pointed out.

"No, I am not. I appear this way—and the chairs appear this way—because *you* are human. You are not ready to see Eternity the way it really is, because when you finally do so, you will see it through the eyes of your Creator—or rather, you will experience it through him.

"Think of it this way: this is your human experience, still tied to existence, your opportunity to understand everything within the limits of your human framework. If you were to come to understand all of it when you are exposed to Eternity, then you would miss experiencing the joy and wonder of its discovery. True, all humans come to understand it completely when they come to Eternity—but you attempted to do it through your book while you were still in existence. You tried to pursue the truth as far as was possible for you.

"So here you are. And here am I, ready to guide you through it. I am also experiencing all of this, and so I am growing in my experience. While I cannot interfere with your creator's work, I have been granted the opportunity to meet with you here, to allow you to see the Artist's work as I see it. In doing so, I am not interfering with his creation because you have already divined—pardon the pun—all of this through the book you wrote. However, thanks to you I will be able to share this encounter with the others here in Eternity who come to experience the Artist's work. I will also show you how I came to be the one to whom the Artist first unveiled his creation, his masterpiece, so that you can experience that event along with me."

I shook my head, still confused. I knew all of this as it was explained to me, but try as I might, I could not recall a single detail of my book beyond each unfolding moment. "Why can't I remember?" I asked in frustration.

He laughed. "So you want to know how the story ends before it has barely begun? What kind of writer are you?"

I smiled and looked up at him under my brow. None of this was how I would have imagined it, yet it was exactly as I had written it. I was, I suppose, experiencing the "film" version of my book—but there was none of the disappointment that often accompanies a film rendition colliding with a reader's imagination. Rather, this was a rendering I could never have experienced in my lifetime . . .

. . . in my lifetime! "Am I dead?" I cried out.

"You certainly don't look like a corpse," he replied jovially. "No, 'dead' is what you'd be after you died in your sleep back in your existence, in there." He cocked his head toward the cloud. "'Dead' is a body after it loses its life. You already know you are more alive now than you ever have been."

He was right. I was alive in every way I had ever been alive, all at once. This was no hallucination; this was more real than any moment I had ever experienced in the foggy now of my existence.

"Okay," I ventured, "so tell me more about you and the Artist and his audience. I was taught the idea of one God, one Creator. How do you—and any others—fit into any of this?"

He smiled. "I know you are confused. So let me sort things out: If I am not human, who am I? For that matter, who are you to me, or to your Creator?

"I am part of the 'great assembly' over which your Creator presides, as referred to in your Bible's Psalms 82, 86, and 89. You have been taught that you should worship only your God, and no other. That commandment never meant there are no others like him; it simply meant that you should worship *only* him. He is the only God and Lord of your world.

"So I am here only to help you understand what your Creator did and how he did it, as the critic. Beyond that, I have no role with you."

I looked around the room that wasn't really a room. "So . . . is this Eternity?"

He laughed loudly. "That would certainly be a disappointment, wouldn't it? No, no, this is just your own idea—the idea of an artist's studio. Like the idea of the critic, you made up the studio as a literary device, a context for the Artist and me, the critic, to discuss his creation—the cloud." He nodded toward that indefinable shape.

"Tell me more about Eternity." I leaned forward on my elbows, curious and ready to learn.

2

Eternity

"THERE'S NOTHING TO IT," said the critic, and then he sat there, grinning.

I threw up my hands in exasperation. "Is this just going to be some kind of game?"

"No," he replied, "I was giving you a serious answer, but I admit I am toying with you a little. Let me ask you this: What have you been taught about Eternity?"

I thought a little. "Well, Eternity has no beginning, no end, no boundaries, and so on. It is infinite, it lasts forever."

He shook his head. "To call it 'infinite' is a bit of a mistake. Something that is infinite is usually described as extending without end, but that idea usually involves some sort of dimension or context—an infinite line, an infinite plane, or an infinite solution to an equation. A term such as 'forever' also fails to describe Eternity, because 'forever' implies time—and time is completely contained within existence and has no meaning in Eternity."

He stood up and spread his hands. "Try this: in mathematics, what number best matches the idea of Eternity?"

I considered his question. What number was big enough? A trillion? A quadrillion? I thought about saying "Infinity," but he had already eliminated that answer. Only one number was unique enough in its properties.

"Zero?" I answered hesitantly.

"Exactly!" he shouted. "If you consider the idea of Eternity as zero, then everything you've ever been taught or imagined about Eternity makes sense: no boundaries such as beginnings or endings, no time, no dimensions, both limitless and incalculable."

"How can something be nothing?" I asked. "Zero is zero—where is there room for anything to exist?"

He snorted. "That term 'exist' is at the root of your inability to comprehend Eternity. Anything that exists had to come from something, according to your science and your experience. What you have to consider is the idea that there is a state beyond existence that is the norm. Your language is based on existence; consequently, there are no words to describe any other states. 'Zero' and 'nothing' connote an absence, but a better term could be 'potential.' Eternity is a state of potentiality—anything can come from it.

"But so too is zero. Consider the number zero and then begin to add to it by subtracting its negative counterpart: take away −1 to get +1, and so on. There is no number, no mathematical relationship, that cannot be pulled from zero if it is balanced by its negation. You can therefore begin to see zero as a *source* rather than as an absence. Zero is not nothing—it is the potential for everything."

I nodded, beginning to understand.

"Likewise," he continued, "zero is achieved by eliminating the mathematical equivalent of existence. Zero is the one number that can only be achieved through subtraction. In mathematics, zero cannot be approached by any non-subtractive methods; you must eliminate the value completely to achieve nothing. Multiplying by zero is the same as subtracting the non-zero factor from itself, and dividing by zero is meaningless. You can divide a number, well, infinitely, but you can never actually get to zero by doing so.

"It's as if there is a barrier around zero that is true of your entire existence—in the sum of your universe and all possible universes—in all of existence, nothing substantive ever completely disappears. It simply changes into other forms—matter into energy, which can then disperse but never cease to exist—similar to what your scientists used to call the law of conservation of matter and energy.

"Your own scientists argue about whether there is a limit to your universe, about whether it is expanding into a void of nothingness, but they never take the nature of that nothingness into consideration—or else they avoid the issue altogether by assuming the universe to be infinite."

He paused, apparently dissatisfied with his own lecture.

"But zero is still not the right idea to express Eternity. It is better for you to imagine all of existence as a sphere—which it is, if viewed as only a product of its greatest probabilities. When viewed as a product of all of its probabilities, it looks like this." He motioned toward the cloud. "Think of existence as a sphere and then look at Eternity as what is beyond the sphere. Unfortunately, that leads us straight back to the traditional ideas of Eternity as infinity or forever—as what extends beyond something, or as time everlasting—and, as I mentioned before, that too is wrong." He shrugged.

"What's particularly wrong with that is that it makes it sound as if existence is the norm, when it is in fact pulled from Eternity. Eternity is the default state. Eliminate existence and you're left with Eternity. Go beyond existence and it is all Eternity. Shrink existence and what fills in the gap is Eternity. Existence can be bigger or smaller than its immediately previous state; Eternity never changes size, regardless of the size of existence.

"So here is a final attempt to describe it: imagine Eternity as zero, and existence as everything on both sides of a number line stretching away from it. Now rotate that number line 360 degrees and you will have described a circle. Rotate that circle, and you describe a sphere.

"But the original number line was infinite in length in both directions, so the circle and the sphere are infinite as well. Since they are infinite, they have no edge and cannot really be described as a circle or a sphere because what you're really envisioning is dimension. Does that make sense?"

When I nodded, he continued.

"For simplicity, let's continue to refer to that infinite dimension as an infinite sphere. Now, instead of looking at zero as a point in the middle of that infinite sphere, imagine turning it inside out. Instead of it all expanding out from zero, imagine it expanding inward. That's difficult for you to do, of course, but if you try, you will probably see the zero as a boundless sphere as well, with existence contained somewhere within it—except that this sphere contains zero, is zero, and consists of zero everywhere it spreads. It is consistent, constant, imperturbable, incalculable, and without dimension or limitation."

He cocked his head and peered at me. "Can you grasp that? Your existence is ever-changing, subject to forces that are not always predictable, and *limited*. It cannot be a constant; it must originate from something else.

"That something else is Eternity—zero—the norm."

Just as I was beginning—only beginning, with no hope of succeeding—to grasp the concept, he interrupted my thinking. "The only reference that approximates Eternity in your existence is the concept of zero. But you and all humans only see zero as the absence of existence. That is as centric as your old idea that Earth was the center of your universe.

"What lies beyond existence is not nothingness. Nothingness is the equivalent of zero, meaning nothing is there. Eternity is the potential for anything and everything—and that is what lies beyond."

I sat there, my mind spinning, trying to comprehend his passionate speech. But then I saw a point. "If Eternity is constant and unchanging, then how does existence come about?"

The critic looked down and shook his head, smiling. "As constant and imperturbable as Eternity is, your Artist found a way to perturb it."

That statement was an open invitation to pursue the question of creation, but I refrained. I still had another unanswered question standing right in front of me.

"So then tell me about all of you who live in Eternity, and tell me about the Artist."

The critic sighed dramatically, though obviously delighted at the invitation. "You are asking me to describe the indescribable, yet you will soon know all the answers anyway. Still, that's why I'm here—and you're not there yet." He clambered back into his oversized chair.

"Artists are especially revered here in Eternity. Before he created *Existence*—the title of this, his masterpiece"—he motioned to the cloud—"your Artist was already renowned. He has the gift to be able to see beyond Eternity, to see relationships where none had been before.

"To enable you at least to begin to understand this, I need to clarify a few points. First, as I mentioned before, there is no such thing as 'time' in Eternity. Time needs matter and space to exist; basically, it needs existence. In Eternity, there is no such thing as time. Once something happens, it has always happened and always will happen. Nevertheless, there is sequence—there is the way things are before something happens, and the way things are after it happens."

He looked at me expectantly. "Yes, I realize I just made two contradictory statements, but bear with me.

"If you stretch your time-constrained mind a little, you may be able to grasp the idea of sequence in Eternity. Think of it as a sphere of experience. Like your creator, I have my own such sphere. No matter where I look from within that sphere, I can see everything at once. The outer layers may have come after the inner layers, but even from far within my sphere, I can still see those outer layers, and I can"—he made air quotes with his fingers—"'occupy' any place within any of those layers.

"It's a bit like living in a growing onion that is completely transparent. As the occupant, I can be at the core or anywhere within it, but I can still see to the core as well as to the outermost layer. Another layer can then be added and it is obviously the newest one, but still visible from the core. Of course," he added hastily, "the metaphor isn't appropriate because we denizens of Eternity have no core, no source.

"But even from the layers of least experience, I can see the layers of greatest experience, and vice versa. The outer layers are greater because they contain more experience than the inner layers."

He continued, "Look at your own life as you see it now, in this state. You are at once a baby, an adolescent, a young man, and an elderly man. That is similar to how I see myself, except I have no beginning and no end like you do. The idea of limitations came from your creator—but more about that later.

"So, if everything is available to me at once, you might ask, then what could I desire? What would motivate me to want anything else? Well, I crave *experience*. I desire a bigger sphere, so to speak.

"My sphere is also my personal expression: it distinguishes me from others, such as your Artist, your creator. It is possible for me to experience something that my peers have not; however, once I interact with any of them, my expression becomes part of their experience, and they know it as well. Still, there is a difference between my experiencing it on my own and their experiencing it through me. I suppose you could call those distinctions 'perspective,' but that is not quite right. In your existence, your perspective is uniquely yours, and no one else can ever completely share it. In Eternity, we all share each other's experiences; there is simply the thread of a kind of identity, of personal context, that weaves through them all.

"That, by the way, is why the Artist—your creator—promised that you would experience Eternity *through* him. It's simply the way we do things here, a completely natural state.

"Returning to my point, perhaps now you can understand why the role of the artist has such importance for us in Eternity. If an artist can give us new ways of looking at things, new means of experience, then that fulfills our fundamental desire."

I nodded. "Okay, I think I can understand all of that. So"—I leaned forward again eagerly—"tell me more about the Artist."

3

Heaven

"WELL, FIRST OF ALL, he *is* an artist," began the critic with a bit of an affected drawl. I must have looked annoyed because he took on a more serious air. "No, that's important for you to take in. You are part of a work of art, his masterpiece, called *Existence*. What you may not realize, however, is that you are not his only work. After all, if you are his 'masterpiece,' then that word implies that there are earlier, lesser works."

Even as his tone became more professorial, I could see the critic relaxing, settling into his established role of explaining an artist and his work. For the first time, however, I realized he looked a little silly, a man sitting in a chair far too large for him, looking like a large, animated doll. It occurred to me that his importance was diminished in taking this form in this setting—it was obviously intentional.

"The earliest works are not important here, since *Existence* is not derivative of them. However, the work immediately preceding yours was critical to the creation of *Existence*." He now looked at me, obviously expecting me to hazard a guess.

"Some other universe?" I felt obligated to give a response, but that was all that came to mind.

"Oh, no, you're still thinking far too—small, that's probably the right term," he replied easily. "You're not just a part of your universe. You're a part of *Existence*—absolutely everything there is, even beyond your simple universe. But I'll explain more about that later.

"No, the earlier work is called *Heaven.*" This startled me a little. I'd never thought about heaven as a creation, although now it seemed rather obvious.

"I guess I always thought heaven was just where God lived," I said.

The critic smiled indulgently. "No, Eternity is his home," he clarified. "You humans do tend to blur the distinctions—heaven, paradise, eternity, the afterlife—but they're not all quite the same thing.

"The Artist became intrigued by the very qualities of Eternity, and *Heaven* was his attempt to make his audience see Eternity a little differently. What made your Artist especially noteworthy— some, like me, might even use the word 'notorious'—was that he took things further than we might have wanted. In fact, he began toying with the very precepts of Eternity, imbuing his creations with qualities that, well, were a bit like ours."

My mind immediately recalled that always intriguing statement from the Bible concerning Adam and Eve: "And the Lord God said, 'The man has now become like one of us.'" I shook my head to clear it and focused again on the critic.

"*Heaven,*" he continued, "the work that established him as a master artist, was the first to feature a setting distinguishable from the rest of Eternity because it actually had dimensions—length, width, height, depth—as well as sequence. It was inhabited by an-gels, creatures who could make choices that were not necessarily the will of their creator. The result was the first epic story.

"*Heaven* itself is part of Eternity, but it occupies a *place*, a lo-cation in Eternity. It is from *Heaven* that the Artist first established the concepts of length, width, height, and depth—and also infin-ity. Unlike dimensions in your own universe, *Heaven's* dimensions have no limitations. Length is infinite distance, width adds infinite plane, height adds infinite space, and depth adds infinite volume.

The Artist introduced the idea of a center, which is what gives the dimensions their definition.

"The creatures of *Heaven*, angels, occupy those dimensions although they have no particular size, no measurements along the dimensions; they are defined by qualities. But they do have a function called *worship*. They are art that can admire itself as art: they are creatures of Eternity and works of art who can appreciate and show gratitude for the artistry of their own creation—their show of gratitude is worship. Through the angels, we first experienced ecstasy.

"The angels are capable primarily of appreciating beauty wherever they see it—and, of course, the greatest beauty is the Artist and what the Artist has created." He paused, then glanced sideways at me with an ironic expression. "Can anything be more beautiful than the source of one's own creation?

"Before *Heaven*, we had not yet experienced beauty. The Artist not only used the perceptions of the angels to allow us to experience the glory of creation, he also introduced into it something that was previously available only to us denizens of Eternity: the ability to make choices. With choice also came the idea of conflict."

He suddenly looked uncomfortable, frowning and rocking sideways a little in his chair with his hands tucked beneath his legs.

"You see, the angels are capable of distinguishing themselves from each other and from the Artist, and that is what led to the conflict in *Heaven*—those who remained devoted to worshipping and serving their creator versus those who chose to glorify and satisfy themselves. Some of the angels chose to focus on their own qualities and beauty, and actually resisted the will of their creator."

He raised his palms and looked at me with consternation.

"I cannot communicate to you how incredibly original—and disturbing—that darker choice was to the Artist's audience. Here we had creatures who could *turn away*—actually *reject*—the will of their creator! Even more fantastic—and, again, disturbing—was the fact that the Artist could do nothing about it! Of course, he could have destroyed them or taken away their freedom of choice—but that would have violated the integrity of the work, the most basic feature of the art. We—and the Artist—could only sit back and watch."

He shook his head. "As a critic, I have to admit that I was disturbed in yet another way by the infusion of choice, for it led me to an emotion I had not previously experienced: a disdain for the selfishly-focused angels. In a way, one could say that there was then a darker side to Eternity, and I was torn between admiration for what the Artist had achieved and a desire to avoid it. I expressed some reservations in my criticism of *Heaven*. Nevertheless, I also recognized the artistic achievement: the concept of conflict had been introduced to Eternity."

The critic paused for a moment, then leaned forward with a grimace and wagged his finger at me. "Art is not always comfortable."

4

The Artist and the Critic

THE CRITIC LEANED BACK in his chair, again raising one leg and grasping his knee. "So you see, your Artist is a bit of a rebel."

I pictured the traditional portrayal of God as an old man with a white, flowing beard, and then pictured him instead as a young artist with dark hair and a challenging gleam in his eye. The contrast was stark and I chuckled.

The critic gave me an appraising look. "I see you are adjusting your perspective a little." He sighed, and added, "All of us had to adjust our perspectives. But your Artist was far from finished.

"I received an invitation from him for the unveiling of his latest work. He told me it was his 'masterpiece.' Given the radical nature of his last work, I was instantly curious and went at once to his studio." He waved his arm grandly around the strange room in which we were seated.

"So this is where he created my world?" I asked.

"Well, not exactly, but yes, you could say that. Again, this is only a rendition to help you understand everything in terms more familiar to you. It helps you comprehend more easily the idea that, as an artist, he had to be somewhere outside of his creations. You humans often perceive him as being somewhere in your skies or space, or in your concept of heaven. Those ideas are completely wrong, although he can of course enter *Existence* or *Heaven*. But more about that later."

He stroked his goatee and became thoughtful. "As I approached the Artist's studio, I mulled the overtone of unusual excitement that had accompanied his invitation. Obviously, he believed that this new work would be even greater than *Heaven*. The prospect of experiencing something completely new thrilled me, but my uneasiness about some of the elements of *Heaven* gave me reason to wonder if my imminent experience would be entirely good.

"As a critic, my job was to be the first to experience the Artist's work." He smiled. "In general, I am a little like the royal taster for a king in your world. If I find the work worthy, then the rest of the assembly will experience it as well. If, for some reason, I find it distasteful—better not to be experienced—then even though the experience is available to the rest of the assembly, they can avoid it. Unfortunately, however, I'm stuck with it."

He gave me a wry grin. "This does not happen often, but I do have a few 'bumps and bruises' that the rest of the assembly—save the unfortunate artists responsible for my less desirable experiences—do not share. Not only can I not avoid those experiences, but they even become part of my personal expression." He chuckled. "I feel a little bit like one of your stereotypical pirate characters—swashbuckling, adventurous, charming in my own way—yet the first thing you notice about me is the patch over my eye."

He noticed me looking at him a little more closely and waved his hand, shaking his head. "No, of course I don't mean that literally. You'd have to see me the way your Artist sees me to understand what I mean about how I express the experiences of the bad art. But don't worry, you'll eventually be able to do that."

"It doesn't sound pleasant," I observed. "So why do you do it? Why be a critic?"

"Well," he replied, "as I stated earlier, new experience is a fundamental desire for the denizens of Eternity. While there are many ways for us to gain new experience, art plays a special role. That is something we have in common with you humans, because art—for you and for me—is an enrichment of perspective and experience."

He shrugged. "What does that mean? Allow me to give you an example. Imagine that all of your universe were one universal shade of green. Would you then be able to see anything?"

"No," I responded. "Of course not! With no contrast, no edges, everything would be the same, and green would be a constant. I suppose that, actually, there would be no difference between infinite green and infinite darkness or light. You can't see something that is always everywhere."

He held up a finger. "Yet there is a way you could see the green—if you could at least *imagine* red." After considering his point, I nodded agreement.

The critic continued, "Contrast is the essence of art, and its ultimate purpose as well. The artist's goal is to keep you seeing, appreciating, even imagining 'red.'

"The fox in your world may use the light of the sunset to find her way, but she does not—cannot—appreciate its beauty. You, on the other hand, can appreciate the contrasting colors and compare it to other such experiences.

"The artist has the special gift to show you aspects of your existence—both real and imagined—that you have never seen or experienced before. In fact, you—and I—judge artists especially by their originality and their ability to engage you in experience. Without artistic perspective, you humans would eventually join the fox in moving through a backdrop world that rarely rises above the functional, in which the only art is that of perpetuation and survival.

"Art provides those of us in Eternity with new perspectives on what we have already experienced. Your Artist, however, has given us new perspectives on the very nature of Eternity. When he created dimensions in *Heaven*, he introduced the concept of *place* or *location*. The stark contrast of that concept to the nature of Eternity brought our attention to features of Eternity which we had not perceived before. When he gave choice to the angels in *Heaven*, he made us aware for the first time of our actual ability to make choices—something we had previously taken for granted."

He sighed and gazed into the distance. "All I could think about as I approached his studio was one question: Would I like what I was about to experience?"

He slid off the chair and gestured to me. "Come, let me use that idea of 'the story' and show you what he did next." I obeyed and approached him, and then had a strange sensation. It was as if I was walking *into* him, as if the distinctions between us were fading.

I heard his voice, but it sounded now more like a voice inside my own head. Suddenly, I was seeing as well as hearing the critic's story.

He began his narrative.

5

Limitations

(THE CRITIC'S NARRATIVE)

As I ENTERED THE studio, I saw the Artist with his head immersed in a large multicolored and glimmering mass, a cloud defying any definition of dimension or shape. For a moment, I simply stared. Everywhere I looked, the cloud eluded focus, seeming to slide off to one side or the other and leaving me with the impression that I was constantly looking at something that had just drifted away. The Artist looked a little ridiculous, his head in the cloud and his lower body bent at the waist, his bottom in the air.

"What is this?" I asked, and the Artist withdrew his head from the mass and looked up at me, startled. He appeared as a handsome young man, with short, dark, and wavy hair and flashing eyes.

Seeing it was only me, he visibly relaxed, smiled, and made a grand sweeping gesture toward the cloud. "This is my masterpiece."

"Masterpiece? This cloud? But it has no form, not even any sense of consistency." I was feeling immense disappointment.

"You aren't seeing it for what it actually is. You're just looking at the outside," explained the Artist. Excitement danced in his eyes. "You have to enter it at least a little to see it for what it is."

"I think you'll have to explain what you mean," I replied, folding my arms and frowning. The Artist smiled, accustomed to my imperious demeanor. He knew that I had been looking forward to this unveiling of his latest work. He, too, had been anticipating this event, the chance finally to reveal his work and provide a completely new experience for his peers.

"What you are looking at is something I call *Existence*," began the Artist. "Notice how, even though it's without form, it nevertheless has boundaries." He paused, enjoying the moment and the consternation he had expected from me. "What if you were to enter into it and become defined by its limitations?"

"Limitations? What are limitations?" I asked, puzzled.

"That's just it!" replied the Artist. "This work, *Existence*, is the antithesis of Eternity. In this work, everything within it faces the possibility of ceasing to be. It changes everything—the very concepts of purpose, of power, of value—they all take on new meaning when they become limited."

Instead of the shock and wonder he expected to see in my face, the Artist saw only confusion. His shoulders slumped. When he had first conceived of the idea of limitations, he had become enchanted with his vision for how such a radical idea would be received. My response fell far short of that fantasy.

Yet he was talking about concepts quite foreign to me. In Eternity, I had never experienced the idea of a limitation or an ending.

Visibly gathering patience, the Artist replied, "Like any art, this work widens our understanding of who we are. You see, I am now part of my art. I have taken on those limitations and allowed them to affect me. Even more, I have drawn from the work its very subjects to share eternity through me." I stared at him, hearing only gibberish.

The Artist paused, watching me for some glimmer of understanding. Seeing nothing, he continued, "When one's very existence is limited, there would seem to be no need to desire to search beyond one's own circumstances. What would be the point?

"The angels I created in my last work, *Heaven*, were part of our Eternity. They glorify me as their Artist, even though they could choose to turn away from me. But unlike us, they do not look to each other to further their experiences; they look only to me."

At last, something made sense! "I warned you about that direction," I replied (a bit smugly, probably—the chance to say "I told you so!" is every bit as appealing in Eternity as it is in *Existence*). "Creations should be subject to their creator; it was very dangerous to give them autonomy." I was warming to my subject, intent on delivering my criticism once again. "I admired that you used the very device of art itself to bind them to you—the artistic elements glorifying the art itself—and I told you that. The idea that a creation could be aware of its creator, have the choice to continue being part of the art, yet would choose to remain because of the artistic quality of its own creation—well, that was a layered irony, I admit.

"I was also fascinated with the concept *of* irony—and conflict, although I voiced some discomfort with it as well. I was concerned about you continuing any further with the creation of that kind of autonomy. It would be a sign of weakness to have to destroy your own work because it does not comply with your intentions. And it is not wise to imbue your creations with qualities you have promised not to control," I concluded firmly, confident of my points.

The Artist appeared unbothered by my reference to our earlier disagreement. "Ah, but right there is the thrill! Please bear with me when I tell you that I *have* gone a step further. Actually, I have gone many steps further.

"But before you react, take a look. This goes far beyond my previous work!" exclaimed the Artist, beckoning me to come closer to the cloud.

I approached the work cautiously, not trying to hide my doubts. The Artist, however, was oblivious, completely focused on his work. "What you see now appears hazy and undefined, and that is its real nature. But what I have done is to create something called 'perception'—depending on how you look at it, you see it very differently.

"In there are creatures who experience what *might* occur as their actual world. They can imagine possibilities and, to some extent, choose what becomes their reality. But, like us, they also possess the ability to imagine things they can't see. As a result, they can upset and even somewhat control the system of probabilities with which they interact."

I shook my head in an attempt to clear it. "I have no idea what you are talking about."

The Artist took a deep and frustrated breath, obviously trying to slow down. "Well, as you know, the essence of art is contrast. However, contrast does not always have to be between things that can be seen; it can also be between what is seen and what is imagined—as with irony, which you now appreciate so well," he said, referring obviously to the aesthetics of his *Heaven*.

I frowned. "So what?"

"Awareness—just as with the angels. Even though my creations are completely contained by their existence, they are *aware* of it because they can *imagine* Eternity. They sense what lies beyond the cloud and long for it."

As comprehension rose, I was shocked at what seemed to be cruelty. "So you taunt them? You offer them possibilities that are beyond their actual grasp? You let them sense what they can never reach?"

"No," replied the Artist softly. "No, I offer them the possible. I have given them the ability to control the cloud, and to enter Eternity."

6

The Creation of Endings

(THE CRITIC'S NARRATIVE)

MY EYES WERE WIDE. "So now you've gone beyond what you did with the angels and completely relinquished control? Are you going too far?"

"Don't worry, it's not out of control," replied the Artist. "It's true that I have limited myself. I've arranged things so that I cannot destroy my work and I cannot with integrity control what is in it—although sometimes my creatures ask me to take control, and so I do. But they can only step out of the cloud and into Eternity through me—and because of what they experience in that cloud, I know that most will ultimately choose my will rather than their own.

"That's why this is my masterpiece. Here, you will see creatures with our own autonomous abilities—reflections of ourselves—who nevertheless bind themselves to me, their creator, of their own volition. Those who choose otherwise will remain within the cloud, unable to leave it—but they will always be capable of changing their minds. There is tragic irony in that their desire to be masters of their own fates, to be their own gods, will keep them from becoming what they desire.

"But I'm getting ahead of myself, and the poor creatures who falter are actually foils for the real focus of my work: the creatures who fulfill what I intended for them." The Artist paused, his brow furrowed in troubled thought, then suddenly seemed to become aware again of my presence. "Come, let me show you."

I walked up next to the Artist, who placed his hand upon my shoulder as we faced the cloud. "Let me explain a few things about *Existence*.

"In Eternity, we desire experience. We are aware of the sequence of developing experience, but once we experience something, it becomes a part of us throughout Eternity. We become aware of not having the experience and then having it—contrast. Sequence is the contrasting element that defines Eternity for us."

"Yes," I replied impatiently, "but so what?"

"Well, I began thinking about sequence and considered how I could contrast it to portray it in art. Finally, I considered a novel idea: What would it be like to *lose* an experience?"

I drew back, surprised. "How could that be?"

"That's just it," answered the Artist with an expression of satisfaction as I finally gave the desired reaction. "I'm talking about it *not* being experienced. And that's how I came up with the idea of *Existence*.

"First, I devised a language of relationship—what the creatures, humans, call 'mathematics'—as the architecture for *Existence*." He proceeded to show me examples of relationships using what is known in *Existence* as arithmetic, algebra, geometry, and calculus. "The entire system emanates from a central point called 'zero,'" he explained. "Zero is the rough equivalent of Eternity.

"I took a particle of Eternity—just a point—and separated its energy into two mutually attractive poles." The Artist touched the tips of his fingers together and then drew them apart, as if he were stretching a band horizontally. "The two poles want to come together and resume their steady state as one point of Eternity; they are mutually attractive. But while we regard them as separated—as

I've presented them to you here in the form of the cloud—three important principles derive from their separation.

"First, there is the energy of their attraction to each other. *Existence* is pure energy that takes many forms as both matter and energy."

"Wait, I don't understand." I waved my hands. "What do you mean by poles? And the energy of Eternity is stable, a constant—we know that—so what are you saying?"

"I didn't change the fundamental state of the energy," replied the Artist. "I simply separated the attractive elements that keep it stable, pulling apart their forces and distancing them from each other. They mirror each other. Were they allowed to snap back together, they would be restored to stability—to zero."

I persisted, "You said you separated the point into two poles that mirror each other, but I see only one cloud. Shouldn't there be a separate, duplicate cloud?"

"There is," he explained. "But since there is no difference between the two poles and how they are treated, they coexist within the same mathematical definitions. A world in one pole has a 'shadow world' in the other, but their expression is precisely the same. The only definition of position is their distance from the point of origin, where the two poles rejoin into one. Since both the world and the shadow world occupy that same distance, they occupy the same position and are therefore indistinguishable from each other.

"Picture a line with sequential numbers and zero in the middle. The numbers stretch infinitely in both directions, as positive numbers on one side and negative numbers on the other.

"Now, imagine rotating the half of that line with positive numbers in all directions at once, and then do the same to the half with the negative numbers. You end up with two coexisting spheres. Yes, they originate from two different points, but because they are infinite in radius, those two different 'centers' become irrelevant. That is why the two existences are essentially one."

He paused, collected his thoughts, and started again.

"So you have already led me to my second principle."

7

A State of Polarity

"Whoa, wait a minute!" As I protested in confusion, I became separate once again from the critic. "I thought this cloud was my universe, my existence. What is he talking about? This doesn't sound at all like the world I know."

The critic nodded in understanding. "Yes, I can see this could seem odd."

"What does he mean by a 'shadow world'? Is he saying there is a parallel universe?" I asked. "Is there a shadow version of me somewhere?"

"No, not the way you mean it," the critic replied. "What he's describing is a kind of tension. Your world—everything that exists—is only there because it's in a balanced state of polarity. The Artist is saying that the cloud exists only because of the possibility that it can stop existing."

He pointed to the cloud. "You and others have entertained the notion before, while you were in *Existence*, that creation itself—that cloud—is just a figment of your creator's imagination, right?" I nodded. "Well, that's basically true, except the cloud isn't imaginary. It exists in a state where if it ever came back into union with the other half of that particle of Eternity, it would cease to exist."

He snapped his fingers. "When I say 'cease,' I mean it would be gone without any trace that it was ever there. So no, it's not like there is a shadow version of you. Think of it more as if there is a shadow of nonexistence for you and everything you know."

He chuckled. "Many of your scientists like to argue that God did not create the universe. What they usually mean is that there is no God. However, he's there, all right. What's true is the rest of that argument, that there is always the possibility of there being no act of creation!" He snapped his fingers again. "Just like that, it could completely cease to be, never existing at all!

"But that's not the plan, and that's not the promise the Artist made to you, his creations. The idea that an artist's work could cease to be wasn't new to me. After all, if the cloud suddenly ceased to be, then it also never existed—no end *and* no beginning, just like everything else in Eternity.

"What was new to me was the idea of something that *had* been there ending yet continuing to have existed—the idea that something was no longer there, and yet there could be no question that it once had been there." He shook his head, looking down at the limitless floor. "We denizens of Eternity had never before experienced endings, terminations, destruction . . . death."

My own thoughts wandered for a moment to the Artist himself. In theory, I had actually been looking at God, in the flesh, as I had followed the critic's story—but there was not really a sense of that. The Artist was just a young man explaining his art. I realized that even the critic's story was just a construct—not at all what I would truly experience if all of this were real.

After all, who could imagine as a spiritual experience that my first glimpse of my Creator had been that of his rear end? I smiled to myself.

The critic looked at me. "Are you ready to continue?"

I nodded, and we folded together again.

8

Probabilities

THE ARTIST PAUSED, COLLECTED his thoughts, and started again.

"So you have already led me to my second principle—distance from the point of origin. If you imagine each possible distance, you'll see that the point and the origin represent two ends of a finite segment, or 'endings.' An ending means that something no longer continues, which we've never experienced in Eternity.

"Those segments introduced limitations: you could trace each pole's distance along a line from its point of origin. Both poles—call one positive and the other negative, although there is no actual difference between them—now stretched outside of and away from the original point of Eternity, and their distance was measurable, at least, in reference to all the other points along the line. From the perspective of any point along that axis of those two polarities, there is a limitation: how far away is it from the point where there is no longer any polarity, the point of origin—zero?"

I shook my head in frustration. "I don't understand. So two points are distant from zero, but that just means they occupy the same line. You led us to understand that idea, of lines as dimensions, in *Heaven*. What do you mean by 'far'?"

Suddenly, two small spheres appeared between us, glimmering like the cloud. The Artist asked, "Where is the center between these two objects?" I pointed at the midpoint of empty space between them. "Yes," responded the Artist. "So tell me: When is there more space between each object and that midpoint? When they are this far apart, or"—he reached out and pushed the two objects farther apart—"when they are *this* far apart?"

I nodded in understanding.

"Note, now, that the two objects occupy end points of either shorter or longer segments," he continued. "This is what I mean by 'limitations.'" He waved his hands up and down on either side in the space beyond each object. "This is a distance with end points. The line they occupy is limited in distance." The objects disappeared.

"Were I to allow the two poles of the cloud to come together, as is their nature, they would cease to be distinguishable by becoming once again simply a point of Eternity. For all points along that axis between the poles, then, the collapse of those poles would be utter destruction; in fact, they would completely cease to 'exist.' Likewise, there is a boundary beyond which the poles have not expanded. These two ends of *Existence*—its very limitations—are defined by the point at which Eternity resumes."

I was still confused. "But I still don't see how it leads to the cloud. What you have shown me could be used to create some lines of relationship between points in the two poles, maybe even some patterns, but everything on both sides of 'zero' would be symmetrical. This"—I turned and spread my arms before the formless cloud—"is anything but symmetrical."

The Artist smiled. "There are only the two poles, or points— the two halves of the original particle of Eternity. However, what you are seeing in the cloud is not just the two points but *all* the possible positions that the two points could occupy. You're looking at the probability that each point is here, there, or over there—all at once."

I frowned. "But how? I mean, the two points *are* somewhere. If I found them, then all those other probabilities would be irrelevant."

"Right! But"—he held up a finger, an expression of pure delight on his face—"consider this: What if I poked you here?" And he shoved the finger into my stomach. "Did I poke you anywhere else?"

I was a little disconcerted by his familiarity, but I muttered, "Of course not. Why would you even ask?"

"Ah, but what if there was a possibility that I had actually poked you—here?" And he poked my nose.

I covered my lower face and backed away, sputtering, "Stop that!"

He then lurched toward me with his finger extended, but I backed away. He drew back, chuckling.

My dignity was wounded, but I tried to keep civil. "What is your point?"

He laughed. "My point is that mathematics also expresses probabilities. I could as easily have poked you in the nose as in the stomach. But what if both events not only were equally possible but also occurred as the same point within a sequence?" His eyes twinkled.

At first, I was only focused on the idea of being poked twice—but then I began to grasp what he was saying. "Wait—no, things either happen or they don't. They can't *both* happen unless they happen in sequence to each other."

He laughed. "Well, I didn't poke you the third time. So what were you reacting to? Nothing happened, but you reacted to the *possibility* of it happening."

He was right.

The Artist held up his hands. "That is what I'm trying to show you. Consider for a moment the idea that what happens next—assuming that I was going to poke you again—could go one of two ways. Then imagine both of them happening and everything that follows in sequence from each. Eternity doesn't involve what *could* happen but only what *does* happen. But this"—he pointed to the cloud—"is everything that could happen once I separated the original particle of Eternity into its two counterparts.

"The cloud is simply an expression of possible distances for the two halves of the split particle of Eternity from their point of origin along every possible dimension. Each is comprised of the relational duality that, when joined together with their counterpart along the opposite polarity, become nothing—or, to put it more accurately, collapse into the previous higher dimension until all collapse back into Eternity."

"But, then, is none of it real? It's all just possibilities?" I asked, still trying to understand.

"You are right," answered the Artist. "In fact, you could say that what you see here isn't even here. In this room, before your eyes, is the possibility that I did nothing at all—the probability of zero."

That clarified nothing. The Artist saw it in my eyes and tried again.

"Look at it this way. If I never split the particle apart, then the probability that it is at the point of origin is 100 percent. Does that make sense?"

I nodded. He went on, "So, if we then assume that I *did* split the particle"—he held two fingers up a hair's breadth apart—"the probability that they are at these two positions is higher than the probability that they are at *these* positions." And he stretched out his arms to either side, fingers still held up. "Still making sense?"

I nodded again. He smiled and then said, "So, if we follow those probabilities wherever they go—that the particles moved along a path a little way out, then altered their paths to their respective left, then up, et cetera, the probabilities grow smaller—all given the 100 percent probability that the particles are actually in their original position, never split at all. As the probabilities grow smaller—out at the edge of the cloud—they approach 0 percent probability. In other words, they approach the condition of Eternity again. The cloud is defined by singularities, the points at which the particle no longer has any probability of existing because there are no reference points for it.

"That is why it looks like a cloud. It is a cloud of probabilities—the varying probabilities that I *did* do something, that I split a point of Eternity. That is also why its edges are so undefined, so vague. Not only are they approaching zero, or Eternity, but their actual final ranges also fluctuate depending upon the chances that they are produced by combinations of higher and lower probabilities."

I stood there, letting his words sink in while my eyes continued to struggle with actually *seeing* the cloud. As soon as I focused my gaze upon any part of it, it simply wasn't there. It was more the impression of it being there, all in the peripheral field of vision.

"It is mesmerizing," I allowed. "But how does it actually work?"

"Bear with me and I'll explain everything," replied the Artist. "But to answer your question, I have to explain how I actually started all of this."

9

A Particle of Eternity

(THE CRITIC'S NARRATIVE)

THE ARTIST CONTINUED, "FIRST, when I split and stretched the two halves of the original particle of Eternity apart, I created energy from their attraction. I ended up with two types of forces: attractive and repulsive. The attractive forces, such as the force that my creatures call 'gravity,' are those which seek to pull everything back to the eternal origin, the original point. The probabilities of all distances from the point of origin along all the dimensional arrays represent a repulsive force that expands *Existence*—in other words, the force I used to separate the two halves of the original particle and the extent to which I did that, nearer and farther, or if you want, the force that keeps the two halves apart. It is the interaction of these probabilities against the attractive forces, derived from the potential energy of the original particle, that create all the energies or forces that form *Existence*.

"All of these forces move along the dimensions of *Existence*; in other words, dimension is an expression of relative distance from the eternal origin, and the forces are the energy produced by those distances. Dimensions are infinite—but as they expand, they represent lower probabilities approaching zero at either end. From the point of origin, they range from probabilities approaching the unified value of 100 percent to the farthest values approaching 0 percent, all without ever actually reaching 100 or 0 percent. The actual value of 100 percent represents the two particles joining back together into Eternity, and the actual value of 0 percent represents all of Eternity beyond the current boundaries of the cloud.

"Since dimension is infinite and energy is constantly in motion, the actual distance of any particle of energy or matter can only be expressed in probabilities. All the energy of *Existence* is derived from that one particle of Eternity, spun out in two halves through the dimensions." He smiled and looked at me, his eyes dancing with enthusiasm. "That whole cloud is produced by one particle, split in half, and the resulting probability that those two halves are anywhere within the cloud along all possible paths from the original point in Eternity."

"You keep talking about 'probabilities,'" I interrupted, "but I'm still trying to grasp the idea that when more than one thing can happen, all of them happen. How does that work?"

"Well, the idea of probabilities goes with choice: I can choose to do something or not to do it. But then the language of relationships I created, 'mathematics,' allows me to render those probabilities into something more tangible. First, let me further explain probability itself."

"Thank you," I sighed, briefly touching my nose again.

The Artist chuckled. "If I must make a choice between two actions of equal merit and desirability, then there is a 50 percent chance I'll make either choice—both chances adding up to a 100 percent probability I'll make *a* choice.

"If you consider that everything is possible in *Existence*, then all probabilities except zero can be expressed mathematically. The chance that you'll appear inside the cloud there as a naked being standing on your head in a whirlpool of gelatin may be 1 in 100,000,000,000,000 or 10^{14}, but it's there."

I must have looked intrigued, because he stopped and frowned. "Except that I've forbidden your intervention, of course, so the probability is actually zero."

He smiled at my disappointment. "There must be some basis for the probability. I can't say there is a probability of something happening if something has never existed. You have no connection to *Existence*, so you can't participate in it—you can only observe it—so there's no possibility of you appearing in the cloud. But back to my explanation . . ."

10

Probability, Particles, and Wave Functions

THIS TIME IT WAS the critic who split us apart and interrupted his story.

"What follows is a discussion using terms only we of Eternity would understand. He talks about the relationship between different layers of experience and such. Since you are not yet privy to the nature of Eternity, we're going to skip that part."

"Okay," I replied, "but explain something to me. I understand probability just as the odds of something happening—like a fifty-fifty chance that when I flip a nickel, I'll get heads instead of tails. You seem to be talking about it as something physical. Am I right?"

"Yes and no. You have to accept what your own quantum physicists have come to embrace: that any probability, however small, *could* happen. There may be only one chance in one trillion that something can happen, but if something happens a trillion times, then eventually that one unlikely event will occur.

"Here's an example. The nickel you are flipping *could* land on its edge one time out of six thousand tosses. That reduces both the heads and the tails probabilities to less than 50 percent each, because there is a small probability that *neither* heads nor tails will happen.

"Now add in the probabilities that the coin doesn't land—or that it only falls partway—or that it keeps on going *up*—which is possible, as I'll explain in a moment. Quantum physicists came to understand, as I mentioned before, that *all* probabilities exist, even if the probability is incredibly low. You see, in *Existence* there is no such thing as 'zero probability' unless it involves something not in *Existence* at all."

"So *anything* could happen? Is there a chance, then"—I began searching my brain for the ridiculous—"that a unicorn could trample me in my living room?"

He laughed. "No, of course not, because there are no unicorns in *Existence*. Probabilities exist only for possibilities that have *some* basis for occurring. But try this: Could you walk through a wall and appear on the other side intact?"

"Of course not," I replied easily.

"Wrong. There is plenty of space between atoms. The chances are incredibly small, but perhaps your atoms could shift around the atoms of the wall so that you could pass through. In fact, your electronic devices would not even work if electrons could not pass through barriers they are not supposed to be able to penetrate."

I knew that. At least, now that he'd explained it, I knew it—but I knew it before, too. Once again, I was reminded that I was my own character, experiencing my own story as I'd written it.

That irritated me, so I challenged him again, mostly out of a momentary feeling of spite.

"But you said earlier that the flipped coin could keep on going up. Isn't that impossible?"

"Not at all. A gravitational flux of some kind could occur, or a magnet could pass overhead unexpectedly—"

I interrupted with a sigh. "Okay, you're going to have to explain probability a bit more."

The critic held out a finger, and on it was a speck of dust.

"Is this a particle or a wave?" he asked.

"Well, it's a particle of course. It's a piece of dirt," I replied.

"You're only half right, and that was a trick question." He smiled and wiped his finger on his pants. "First, that was just a particle of dirt. But it's made up of the smallest bits of matter that are also called 'particles' by your scientists—protons, neutrons, electrons. Put together as that piece of dirt, it was indeed a particle while you were looking at it. But it also exists as a wave."

"A wave? A wave of what?" I asked.

"A wave of probability. But hold on," he exclaimed as he saw me becoming confused. "Here is an easier way to understand it.

"When you were in elementary school in your time of existence, you were taught that the atom looked like a nucleus of protons and neutrons with electrons orbiting around it, like this." An oversized cartoon atom suddenly appeared between us.

"That depiction of an atom is wrong, however. In reality, what you would see is electrons appearing as a shell around the nucleus. If we cut it in half, it would look like this." He waved his hand over the image and another appeared. It had a core of particles surrounded by a cutaway shell. Where the shell had been cut away was a depiction of orbiting particles.

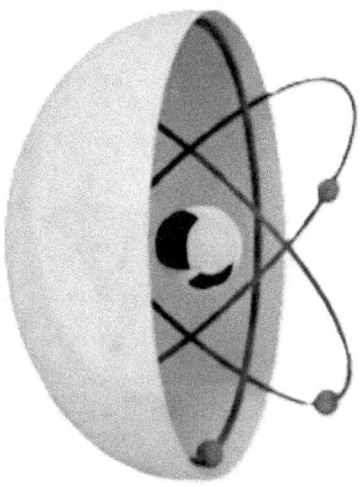

"The electrons form a shell of *probability*—the probability that the electron is in any particular position at any given time. The shell is every possible position and path that the electron could take.

"If, however, we were to identify the actual positions of three electrons around a nucleus at a given moment, the shell would collapse, and we would perhaps see this." He waved his hand again and the shell disappeared, leaving only the particles in the nucleus and three particles frozen in their orbits.

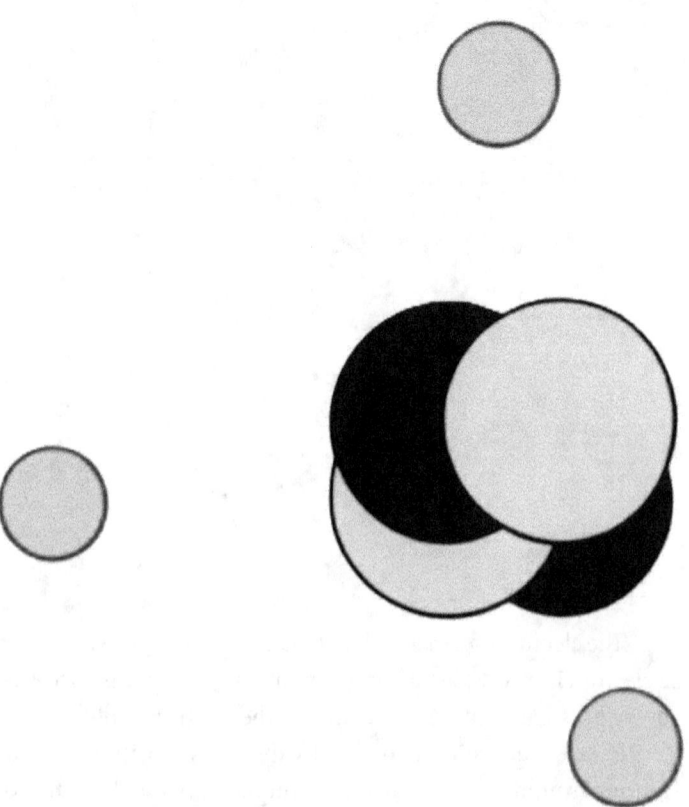

He waved his hand once more and the image disappeared. "In other words, you can calculate the velocity of a particle, but you do not know exactly where it is. You can only calculate the chances that it is in this position, or that position, or some other position. Humans call that 'the uncertainty principle.' These probabilities are represented by a wave function, which I will explain further a little later. Rather than a particle, what you actually have is a wave, just like light or sound is a wave.

"However, if you do identify its exact position by, say, trapping it and observing it, then the wave function collapses, and you have an actual particle. So you were right when you said the speck of dirt was—*at that moment while you were observing it*—a particle. To use the term 'particle' more scientifically, however, let's pretend that the particle of dirt was in fact a particle of matter, like a proton or electron. Obviously, while it is fixed in space on my finger, it can't be anywhere else. There is now no way to calculate its velocity because it isn't moving, and there is no probability that the particle could be somewhere else now that you've collapsed its probability wave function."

The implications of his explanation suddenly hit me. "Wait a minute! So you're saying that while I'm observing something, it becomes a particle, but when I look away, it becomes a wave?"

"That is roughly correct," he replied.

"But then the world only exists when I'm looking at it?" Suddenly, the critic seemed crazy—or worse, maybe *I* was crazy.

"Well, not exactly. Usually when we think of observation, we imagine a *person* looking at something. But whenever anything interacts with something else, that is an observation. Here in this studio, I can produce a speck of dirt, and the only observers are you and me. In your existence, everything interacting with that speck—people, animals, insects, bacteria, or even cameras—are observers. It's rather difficult for something to be unobserved.

"However, each act of observation affects the particle. The reason you saw the speck of dirt is because light is bouncing off the speck and then the unabsorbed spectrum of light enters your pupil. That you absorb that light affects the environment, and therefore, in miniscule ways, the speck of dirt."

A setup of screens suddenly appeared between us.

"Here is an experiment that scientists do in *Existence* that demonstrates how observation affects your world. You have a screen with two slits. We want one particle of light—one photon— at a time to move through a slit, so we'll use a photon gun. As each photon flies through a slit and strikes the final screen—which we'll call the observing screen—it leaves a white mark. This, then, is what you would expect to see after firing the gun for a while." I watched as little beads of light flew from the gun through the slits and impacted the final screen.

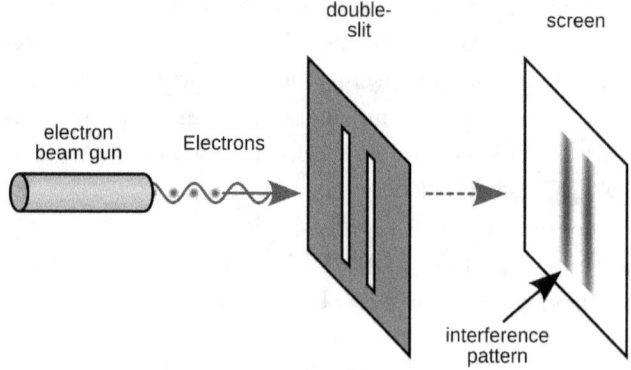

"You would expect to see two bands of light like this, the same as if you shone a flashlight through the slits.

"However, that is *not* what you would actually see. You would see this." The two bands of light disappeared, and instead I now saw multiple bands of light and darkness on the observing screen.

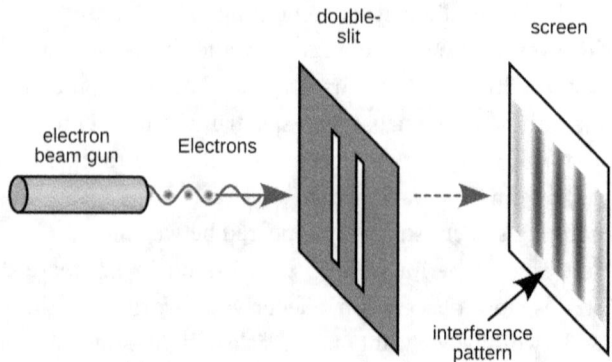

"You would see the two bands of light if the light consisted only of particles. But since the photon consists of *waves*, you see these multiple bands of light. That is because the light is moving through the two slits much like water would. If it were water moving through the slits, the waves would pass through each slit and expand again on the other side.

"Just like water, as the photon—or light—moves through the slits, it expands its possible pathways on the other side. The waves from each slit collide with each other. Where their peaks meet, they become stronger, so the wave becomes stronger—in this case, brighter, so you get the white bands. Where a wave peak collides with a trough, they cancel each other out, and you get the dark bands. But since the waves also overlap, you get multiple bands—an interference pattern."

"But you said the photon is both a wave and a particle," I objected.

"No, I said the photon is a wave until you *observe* it," he replied. "We're using a photon gun instead of a regular light because we want to be able to identify individual photons. Right now, you don't know where the particles of light are. Each photon could be passing through the left slit or the right slit—so the probability that it is passing through either is roughly equal.

"Since you don't know for certain which slit each is passing through, you're seeing all of them as waves—the waves of probability for where each photon is moving. The same photon is passing through both slits at once as waves and ending up as multiple bands on the observing screen.

"But if we were to use a device to tag and identify which slit each photon is passing through—so there is no longer the possibility that it is passing simultaneously through the *other* slit—then *this* is what you would see."

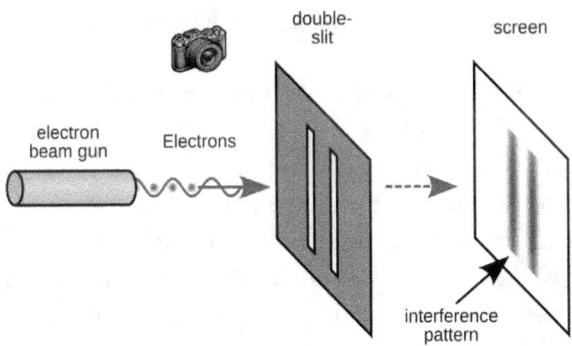

double-slit

screen

electron beam gun

Electrons

interference pattern

I nodded as I looked at the phantom illustration in front of me, where the final board showed two bands of light again. "Okay, I get it. Once we 'see' the individual photon, then there is no possibility it is anywhere else but at that slit at that moment. Since it is no longer a wave—because it doesn't have any probability of being anywhere else—we see it as a particle. It then passes through its slit and strikes the observing screen. Since all the particles are being 'seen' and are passing through only one of the two slits, we get only the two bands of light." I felt somewhat smug in my new comprehension.

"That's right!" The critic appeared proud of his pupil. "Another way of looking at it is quite simple. Imagine a car flashing past you so fast that you see only a blur, like you were close to the track at the Indianapolis Speedway." Suddenly, I was standing in the front row of the bleachers at the speedway behind the protective fence as a race car sped by, sounding like a loud and angry bee. "You could use an instrument to determine how fast and in what degree of direction relative to the track borders it is moving." The sights and sounds of the speedway fell away as suddenly as they had appeared, and I was back in the studio.

"But snap a high-speed camera at the car and look at the picture." I now saw before me a photograph of the race car frozen just beyond the fence. "Based only on the picture, how fast and in what direction is it moving? You can no longer tell, because you only have a still picture. Was it moving toward its left or right? Forward or backward? At 160 miles per hour or 200? Or could it have been stopped completely? That is basically the difference between the wave and the particle states."

The photograph vanished, and the critic held up a pointed finger. "But what you have to understand is that *all* matter and energy have these properties. And the probabilities extend far beyond your immediate proximity. If you could see yourself in your wave form, you'd be a fuzzy being of high probability with gradations extending out in all directions, fading in intensity as the probabilities lower, but extending everywhere into your universe.

"But your wave form isn't actually 'real.' What is real is what is observed—you where you really are, doing what you're really doing, with all other probabilities eliminated.

"Got it!" I replied. "But I'm not sure how we get from that to this." I spread my arms wide and pivoted once. "How do we get, well, everything I know?"

The critic smiled. "Let's find out." He beckoned to me, and we folded together yet again.

11

Fields

(THE CRITIC'S NARRATIVE)

THE ARTIST WAS NOW explaining how he began to create his work. "*Existence* started from a single point, or particle, of Eternity. I split the particle in two, which created two poles that were attracted to each other. That polarization produced energy—the energy generated by the attractive force pulling the two poles back together. Let's call that 'split A.'

"Think of the two halves of the particle as 'positive' and 'negative.' Everything I do with the positive half is mirrored in the negative half. However, merging anything on the positive side with anything on the negative side takes us back to zero or Eternity—so, for that reason, we are going to ignore the negative side for the rest of this discussion. Just think of it as a 'shadow' *Existence*.

"The probability of the positive half of the original particle being at any distance from the original non-split point of Eternity is highest at points closest to the origin, and lower at points farther away. The strength of the attraction diminishes as the probability decreases. In other words, the farther away the positive particle is from the point of origin, the lower the attractive energy pulling it back to the point of origin."

He studied me for a moment, gauging my comprehension. Apparently satisfied, he continued.

"There is an axis of separation between the point of origin and the positive particle. I took every point along that axis and split them all again into negative and positive halves. We'll call this 'split B.'

"Every point of split B represents a different level of attractive energy. Then, as the split B halves move apart, they, too, weaken in their attraction to their opposite halves as they become more distant. This time, however, we are going to keep track of both halves, the positive and the negative.

"All the negative halves emanating out from the split A axis are repelling each other. All the positive halves are also repelling each other. So now we have two kinds of energy: attractive and repulsive." When he saw I still understood him, he nodded and smiled.

"Now it gets complex. I took each split B half, both positive and negative—all of them along both sides of the split A axis—and split them again. We'll call this 'split C.'

"All positives in split B and in split C repel each other, all negatives repel each other, all positives are attracted to negatives, and vice versa. However, split A particles have stronger forces than split B, while split B forces are stronger than split C, and so on—all because of their relative distances from the point of origin. The attraction between a split C negative and a split A positive will be weaker than, say, the attraction between two split A particles because of their respective distances from the point of origin.

"You can now envision how complex the resulting web of attractive and repulsive energy can be. It's a mixture of both the relative strengths and the relative natures of the different levels of split."

To my own surprise, I was still following him. I could envision this vast and ultimately infinite spiderweb of attractive and repulsive energies of varying strengths among particle halves from different split levels. "I can see it," I said.

"Well, take all of that and then imagine that I continue to split each level again and again. Consider the interactions of these different particle halves between each other and between the different levels and think of those interactions—both attractive and repulsive—as 'tensions.' They also overlap with each other. Some of these tensions cancel each other out, while others combine to form tensions of varying natures.

"All of these tensions are what the scientists of *Existence* call 'fields.' Ripples in these fields will manifest as actual fundamental particles in their universe, which can combine to produce all the various matters, energies, and forces they know. Of course, all these tensions were produced originally far beyond their own universe, and their own universe is a product of the intersection of only relatively few of all these fields.

"But there is no fixed point for any particle, so the probabilities take the form of waves. Each wave expresses the probability that the particle is at a particular point from its origin. The farther it is from the origin, the lower the probability. Those furthest probabilities never actually reach zero, but as their differences become infinitesimal, the sphere—or, rather, the shape of all its probabilities, which can be uneven—is defined by an indefinite, or fuzzy, edge."

12

Probability and Dark Energy

"WAIT A MINUTE!" I cried as I broke from the critic. "I remember now! There are two types of fundamental particles, the fermions and the bosons—and those can be thought of as either particles or as ripples in their respective fields. I don't know how many there are, but I do know there are not an infinite number of them."

The critic held up a warning finger. "You are thinking about what he's describing from your perspective as part of your own universe. In other words, you are thinking from the inside out. But *Existence* was created from the outside in. Your universe is only a small part of the overall cloud, a specific place where the intersections of certain fields formed just the right physical laws for you to exist. But there is much, much more beyond your universe that you cannot see.

"As the Artist creates each level, he is creating this cloud in front of you." He pointed at the cloud. "The three dimensions of your universe were produced within many other, higher dimensions."

"But what keeps it all from collapsing?" I asked. "That's what I don't get. If every point in the cloud is being pulled back to the point of origin, why doesn't it all just come together?"

The critic replied, "Well, to some extent, as the Artist explained, because of probability itself." He gestured toward the cloud again. "You're not looking at a cloud of reality based on the fact that the Artist actually split a particle of Eternity. You're looking at the *probability* that he split it. So every subsequent split and all the probabilities of where the split halves are—well, they are just probabilities."

He chuckled. "Probability itself is what keeps the cloud existing. As long as there is any chance that the Artist split the original particle, there is *Existence*. In that whole cloud, no probability is 100 percent. The only 100 percent probability is that he didn't split the particle at all, and there is no *Existence*."

"So I'm not real?" I asked, somewhat sardonically.

"You are, but only in there," he replied. "In the cloud, there is a better than 0 percent chance that you exist." He laughed.

"Probabilities are, by definition, uneven," he continued. "If I assume that an event of low probability occurs, then all the highest probabilities are recalculated to emanate from that lower probability event.

"For example, let's return to the coin toss scenario. Let's say you and I are competing to decide who is going to drive us to a concert. We flip a coin, and I choose heads, but it lands on tails. You win, so you're the one who drives in your car. We don't know it, but the highest probability now is that we will arrive at the concert safely.

"But if I choose heads and it lands heads, then I win, and I'm the one who drives my own car. We are unaware that my brake line is leaking, so now the highest probability is that we will encounter some difficulties—possibly disastrous—on our way to the concert.

"And if the coin lands on its edge, we may be so excited to show it to others that we end up not going to the concert at all, and my brake failure happens tomorrow, when I'm driving by myself." He shrugged. "This least probable alternative—the one-in-six-thousand occurrence of the coin landing on its edge—will realign probabilities when it does occur. Even though it was least probable, it happened—and now reality coalesces around it with what is most probable to occur next, on down to the least probable outcome."

He sighed dramatically.

"We can keep discussing the principle of probability, but in the parlance of your own existence, we'd be wasting time. You should simply accept this truth: at the time of your own personal existence, your quantum physicists had already determined the existence of 'probability waves' in your universe.

"One of your greatest physicists, Albert Einstein, also first proposed the idea of a 'cosmological constant' to counterbalance gravity itself, so that all of your universe doesn't just collapse in upon itself. That cosmological constant later became associated with 'dark energy,' the most pervasive and greatest source of energy, which propels your universe to expand beyond the attractive forces of gravity.

"Dark energy can also be described as the creation of space. Space itself is 'pixelated'—it breaks into individual quanta, so that if you could possibly see it in its quantized form, it would look pebbly. As new space is created, matter is distanced farther from other matter. At the level of your everyday life, though, the other forces, such as the strong nuclear force within atomic nuclei that holds them together and electromagnetism, can overcome the spreading out of space. Gravity itself can also do so when it bends space around objects closer to each other, like in your solar system. But beyond the solar system, dark energy dominates weaker gravity and pushes galaxy clusters farther apart by creating space between them.

"Dark energy is also a clue to the contrast between Eternity and *Existence*. Dark energy makes it impossible to achieve nothingness in *Existence*, because dark energy is always there, all-pervasive. As space is created, dark energy is also created—one of the reasons why the law of conservation of matter and energy has been abandoned by your scientists. Just as all energy and matter was originally drawn from probabilities, so too is space and dark energy.

"Dark energy, energy, and matter are a partial manifestation of the repulsive forces created when the original particle was split. Gravity, however, is the manifestation of the attractive forces of all the splits that ultimately want to pull everything back together into the original particle of eternity—back to zero."

He suddenly reached backward and pulled himself up into his chair.

"Obviously I can't disclose new principles of physics to you." He laughed. "That's for two reasons. First, you can't return to *Existence* with new knowledge that would change everything; after all, I'm not allowed to interfere with anything in *Existence*, and giving you that information would be interference.

"Second," he said, then smiled—pardon the pun, but I can't help it—devilishly, "you're writing the script. I can't tell you any more than you already know or can conceive."

I groaned, and he laughed again.

Probability

WE ALL WALK AMONG each other, secure in our perceptions that we are encased in reality. Yet emanating from us are waves of possibility expressed as degrees of probability.

The woman turns the corner and enters the boutique, and billions of light-years away on a cold, barren hunk of rock orbiting a faded red star, a subatomic particle flickers into existence—one of the very particles of her body's mass—and then winks out.

The probability of what we would normally consider to be impossible events are in fact very low, but they are never zero. In our everyday lives, in which we see only the monstrous shapes of things, we rarely, if ever, see an event of low probability—but at the subatomic level where billions of life-spans are begun and completed in the space of only one of our seconds, the improbable odds that something will occur are in fact met with great frequency.

In an alleyway, a boy tosses a pebble and hopes it will land in a can ten feet away. The odds that it will land on the edge of the can and remain that way are astronomically small—but if he were to toss the pebble as many times as the established odds, then, at least once, that event would happen.

At the subatomic level, the odds that an electron will spontaneously disappear on one side of a barrier and simultaneously materialize on the other side are also astronomical—but the number of times that event's opportunity occurs reaches the odds in less than a second of our perceived time, and therefore actually occurs with regularity.

As you move your arm, every possibility exists. Your arm could continue to move in the same direction, or it could stop, or it could move in a different direction. Every possibility constitutes a universe of related outcomes and probabilities, but then you choose and only one universe becomes reality.

We are space and dust with destinies.

13

Universes

THE CRITIC LEFT HIS chair and motioned for me to fold together with him again, but I didn't move.

"Sorry, I just need a minute to process," I explained, looking down and shaking my head.

"That's fine," he replied easily. "Do you need me to explain anything?"

I thought for a moment, and then said, "Actually, I probably need everything explained, but I'm sure that's coming. But here is a specific question: If all the fields are infinite, doesn't that make the universe infinite?"

He appeared delighted with my question. "Very good! Perhaps I need to clarify one important concept.

"That cloud"—he inclined his head toward the glimmering immensity—"represents all probabilities for existence, for everything that you know in your world and much further beyond. Your universe is not the only one, but it is the only universe that is *real*.

"You will soon find out more about what creates reality, so let me simply address what constitutes a universe. Imagine it this way."

Suddenly, a collection of bubbles appeared before me.

"Imagine each of these bubbles as individual universes," he explained. "Now add the fields that create the fundamental particles, such as quarks and electrons. For the sake of simplicity, let's think of them as two-dimensional planes, even though they actually extend in every direction and occupy every point."

As he spoke, differently colored transparent sheets appeared stretched in all directions, penetrating every bubble at different angles.

"As you can see, those bubbles intersect and contain portions of all the fields, while the fields themselves remain infinite. Each universe is a product of probabilities, and its boundaries are defined by the range of probabilities associated with that universe.

"Your universe is also a bubble, so your universe is indeed finite.

"The mistake is to assume that there is only one infinite universe that contains everything, including the fields. If your universe were in fact infinite, then all probabilities would become manifest somewhere within it." He waved a finger at me. "Then where would your science be? Any possible outcome of any possible experiment would exist somewhere in your universe. What a mess!" He shook his head in feigned astonishment.

"So there are multiple universes, then!" I exclaimed.

He grinned. "Nope."

I was confused. "But you just said . . ."

He laughed. "I said your universe is the only one that is real." He put an arm around my shoulder. "Let's get back to my story and see if it makes sense to you."

14

Collapsing into Reality

(THE CRITIC'S NARRATIVE)

THE ARTIST WAS BECOMING even more animated, his dark eyes flashing. He was pacing back and forth and gesturing at the cloud.

"The cloud will appear as a sphere when viewed through a selected line of probability. If, near the origin, I select a particular probability as reality—identifying the position of the particle and therefore collapsing the wave function—I am then confronted with a new sphere of probabilities for where the particle could go next. As I continue to choose probabilities, I move farther from the origin in a line."

"Hang on," I interrupted. "Slow down and explain what you are saying a little more clearly."

He stopped pacing, took a breath, and began again.

"Usually, in *Existence*, you would expect only the most probable events to occur." He swept his hand before him and an image appeared with movement in it. "Here you see a young human, a boy, using what is called a 'bat' to hit a ball as it flies past him."

I leaned forward a little, intrigued by my first glimpse of *Existence*. "Why is he doing that?" I asked.

The Artist chuckled. "Never mind that right now. You'll understand once you actually see my creation.

"But now you see him swing the bat at the ball and miss. He tries again, and this time something a little less probable happens: he hits the ball." I watched as the boy's bat struck the ball, knocking it out of the image.

The Artist continued, "An even lower probability might be that he not only hits the ball but, through a weird configuration of circumstances, hits it farther than anyone else has ever done before. As the wave functions collapse to this new event, new probabilities come into play based upon what was once unlikely but is now reality." He snapped his fingers and the image disappeared.

"If only the most probable always occurred, the cloud would be mostly evenly shaped and fairly symmetrical. But sometimes the *least* probable occurs, and the cloud expands in its bumpy fashion because we are now much farther out from the origin.

"In other words, the center of the cloud represents the most probable, the edges the least probable. When less likely events occur, that point in the cloud becomes surrounded with the most probable events emanating from it and again stretching out to the least probable events to come from it."

"I think I understand," I replied. "Each event produces an even sphere of possible outcomes, but the actual outcome produces its own sphere of possibilities. You end up with spheres constantly growing out of other spheres, resulting in this lumpy cloud."

"Yes. What you are seeing here are all the possible spheres at once, since no particular probability wave function has collapsed. Because of all those possible overlapping spheres of probability and because of the evolving new probabilities, it appears as a shapeless cloud. That is why," the Artist concluded, "from outside the cloud, you can't seem to focus on any part of it. It's odd, isn't it, not being able to look at it directly? It just slips away, as if it wasn't ever there, and yet you still can see that it's there."

"Yes, it's quite . . . well, actually, it's a little annoying," I replied, still trying to stare directly at the cloud. The Artist chuckled.

"I am intrigued with how you created *Existence*, but I still don't see how this leads to the creatures you mentioned earlier," I continued. "So far, all you have are waves that, if I understand you correctly, can't even be fixed in place because they are only probabilities. What turns the possible into the real? What causes a wave function to collapse?"

"You understand me perfectly." The Artist smiled warmly, obviously pleased with my insights. "Somehow, something besides me alone had to choose a probability as the final reality, to turn a set of waves within all the fields to particles fixed within specific dimensions. I chose to render the reality within three dimensions and develop it along the fourth. Reality would be shaped by movement away from the origin—what the creatures in *Existence* call 'time,' similar somewhat to our sense of sequence. But what could I use to make that choice, to fix reality in place?"

(INTERLUDE)

I stepped away from the critic and spoke one insightful word: "What?"

He smiled. "The Artist is trying to explain how he gets from what *could* happen to what actually does happen. Think about it for a moment: at first, all he has is a lot of energy spun into an incredibly intricate web of energy fields. How do we get from that to the first particle—much less a planet or even a human?

"Let's narrow the discussion down to just your own universe. First, here is an example of a simple waveform." He used his index finger to draw in the air, and as it moved up and down, a line appeared where it had been, creating a floating image.

63

"Since all probabilities exist, the opposite of any probability also exists, and therefore existence never gets started." He drew a mirror image of the waveform below the original.

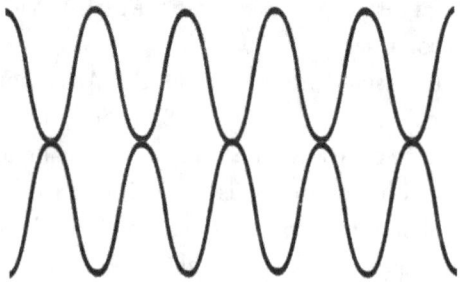

"The wave functions just keep canceling each other out—every point in one wave is matched by an opposite point in the other wave—like −2 + 2 = 0." He put his hands above and below the two waveforms, flipped one over the other, and they disappeared.

"However, since these are wave functions of probability, they also exist in greater or lesser degrees of probability. For example, as you move your arm to the right with great energy, the highest probability is that your arm will continue to move to points further to the right—but there is also the probability, less likely, that your arm will suddenly move to the left. Usually, of course, the highest probability wins. Sometimes, however, a highly improbable possibility wins out, and wave functions go out of sync—creating the unevenness that results in things getting *started*; without it, existence wouldn't—well, exist." He again drew through the air with his finger, tracing one waveform and then adding another over it that didn't match up to the first.

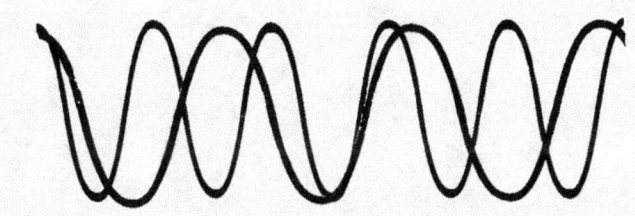

"When wave functions go out of sync, there is nothing to cancel them out. They are now ripe for becoming reality—if the wave function can be collapsed." He swept his hand across the floating image and it vanished. "When your universe was spun into existence, the uncertainty principle caused ripples—uneven waves of probability that sometimes fail to cancel each other in space, which eventually coalesced into your galaxies."

"Okay, I think I follow," I responded. "But what collapses them? We talked about observation making waveforms collapse. But who observes them? The Artist himself?"

"No, it wouldn't be as much fun if the Artist did any more than set the ball rolling by splitting the original particle and then making the resulting halves continue to split," answered the critic. "The answer is that at first the wave functions *don't* collapse. They just keep on generating more probabilities, ranging from the most probable to the least probable. But if you follow those 'improbabilities' far enough, you get an observer, and the wave functions begin to collapse into a reality.

"But I'm explaining too much. Let's go back to hear how the Artist explains it."

Again we stepped toward one another, and again I had that strange sensation of folding into him . . .

15

Life and the Nature of Reality

(THE CRITIC'S NARRATIVE)

"SINCE *EXISTENCE* IS MADE up of probabilities," said the Artist, "there are already possible realities that are the results of lower probabilities—even near-impossibilities—that have disruptive impact upon what otherwise would be never-ending symmetries. Again, these probabilities are expressed as wave functions.

"Thus, any kind of universe that results from even the least likely probabilities can exist. But those universes exist as probabilities, not realities. At this stage, you can imagine all of *Existence* as a multiverse of mathematical possibilities—but none of them are a reality."

I nodded, but I was aware that he had not yet answered my question about getting from the possible to the real.

"Something else," he continued, "had to be introduced to convert probability into reality—to convert matter from wave forms into energy or matter particles fixed in time and space. That something"—he paused dramatically—"is life."

By now, I had established for him a firm pattern of failing to respond to his moments of drama. His excitement changed to annoyance as he looked at my blank expression. Still, he tried again.

"The creatures who are the focus of my work—humans—are always asking the question 'How did life come into existence?'" That is actually the wrong question.

"The better question is, how could life *not* come into existence?

"Life is what translates probability into reality. The odds of the right conditions coming together to form life—those odds are incredibly low. Less than a hair's breadth of complex conditions must line up perfectly for life to happen.

"But the chemical creation of life does have some degree of probability—and the only reality that can come into existence is that dictated by life. Mathematically, the odds of life forming from the chaotic formation of matter are infinitesimally small—but the prospect of life forming in any reality is inevitable. Without life, there *is* no reality."

The Artist turned to me. "Imagine that two rocks floating in space collide with each other. How predictable do you believe the outcome would be?"

I considered his question in light of the mathematics he had shared with me earlier. "It would be quite predictable," I replied, "barring any of the improbable fluctuations you mentioned earlier."

"Correct!" He beamed, his faith in me somewhat restored. "Even with matter and energy coming into existence through those fluctuations, very few truly interesting things happen. It's just matter and energy floating around, forming larger lumps of rock or concentrations of heat.

"But one of the most improbable outcomes is that chemicals and energy produce the phenomenon called *life*. Even more improbable is that this life survives and propagates. But those low probabilities do exist, and so it does happen."

"But what is this life?" I asked. "What makes it different?"

He smiled. "A rock does not have any sense of its environment. But as conditions progress, there come creatures—collections of matter and energy that can store and process energy to reproduce themselves—who are also capable of using the attractive and re-pulsive forces to locate themselves within the overall cloud: life. In other words, they are able to perceive themselves at any given point within *Existence* in relation to all the other probabilities.

"They have several ways of doing this, abilities humans call 'senses.' A creature can sense its context or environment, thereby interacting with it, and when it does so, it becomes an observer: all the waves of probability involving its relationship to the origin point essentially collapse. It can now locate itself within four di-mensions: it has a fixed distance relative to all other energy within *Existence*—that gives it a location within the first three dimen-sions—and a fixed distance relative to the origin—that gives it a location within the fourth dimension, time.

"These senses are made up of stronger and weaker repulsive forces. The very act of interacting with its environment disrupts that environment by collapsing probabilities into fixed points. Any creature with this ability is therefore endowed with what my crea-tures call 'life.'

"However, some creatures can do more—"

(INTERLUDE)

I had to pull away. This was all going too quickly, and my head was spinning. I also sensed that the critic was not about to ask the Artist for any clarification, and I needed some badly.

"Hold on a minute!" I stammered, closing my eyes and shak-ing my head. "He's going too fast, and this is too important. I've never heard life defined this way."

The critic pulled himself up into his chair, clasped one knee, and waited.

"So, let me see if I have this right. Life starts out as storing energy?"

"No, not quite. That's just a transitional stage. You can imag-ine a film of material over the face of a rock by a hydrothermal vent in the ocean floor, a film that is capable of absorbing and storing energy. A battery can do the same thing, but it's not life.

"Rather, it starts becoming life when it metabolizes the energy—when it starts adding to itself by converting that energy into matter."

"Okay, fine. I remember reading some stuff from biologists theorizing about something like that being the means by which life got started. I also read about 'chemical soups' getting started by lightning." I looked at him for a response, but he just smiled and shrugged.

I decided to move on. "But what was all that about senses?"

"Ah, that was the key point!" the critic exclaimed. "It's one thing when two rocks collide in space—physics can explain how they'll react nearly every time. But it's quite another matter when one thing can sense what it is about to come into contact with. That film on a rock that I mentioned earlier, for instance—maybe it grows toward where the energy is hottest. After a while, it can actually detect where energy is hotter. What happens when it can sense it's on a rock? And that another nearby rock has a better angle for getting to the heat?

"If something like that can sense that moving or growing in a particular direction will improve its situation, and it does so, then what it has actually done is *perceive* probabilities and *choose* one probability. Life can be defined as having the ability to sense probabilities and to make choices—even the less probable choice."

I considered what he had said. "That actually makes a lot of sense. Along with the ability to metabolize, I guess it makes a pretty good definition for life.

"But wait a minute. He said that when a form of life makes an observation—perceives something with its senses—then that creates reality by collapsing the wave functions of probability. I get that, but whenever a creature makes a choice, it creates a new reality. Right?"

"Right," replied the critic.

"But then, that means there are *two* realities, right? One where the creature made that choice, and one where it *didn't*. Both realities are being perceived by living creatures."

"No, not right," said the critic. "That would result in an infinite number of realities, and any reality becomes more or less meaningless since all the other realities also exist.

"No, your Artist was cleverer than that.

"Reality always follows the sum total of the observations and choices made by life. When a creature makes a choice, that choice determines the reality both for it and for the other creatures in proximity to it—at the same time that the choices made by the other creatures determine the first creature's reality. Reality results from a kind of natural consensus, somewhat like pool balls colliding on a table and forming a constellation. The possibilities not chosen remain probability wave functions, not reality."

I stood there, taking in the concept. Its sheer complexity was overwhelming, even though the concept itself was simple. "So all life contributes to reality at all times? It seems like an incredibly complex Venn diagram—reality is in the space where all perceptions overlap."

"Correct." The critic beamed, obviously pleased with my performance as his student. "In that cloud"—he twisted a little to look at it—"is a thin thread of reality, so thin it would be the equivalent of a single line of atoms in your reality. Everything else is just probability.

"Observations are not made only by life, but until life comes along, there is no reality. Life can make choices, and non-living things cannot. A rock that falls on you certainly causes waveforms to collapse in unfortunate ways, but the rock didn't choose to fall on you. However, a rock crashing into the ground in a universe without life is a meaningless phenomenon. Until something alive comes around to observe the crater, the event has no reality. Before life, there is only the cloud of probability. But once life begins, so too does reality.

"Every choice you make has to align with the realm of probabilities for every particle in your body, as well as the realm of probabilities for every particle in your physical environment, and also the choices being made by every living creature in your environment. Then imagine that entanglement of choices and probabilities emanating outward from your immediate environment to neighboring environments and so on throughout your world. All of it has to reconcile instantaneously. The phenomenon that your scientists call 'entanglement' is an example of that kind of instantaneous reconciliation."

I shook my head, trying to imagine it all. "So my decision to move my arm has an impact on what happens everywhere in the universe?"

"No," replied the critic, "not really. Moving your arm doesn't necessarily affect any of the probabilities on, say, the planet Mars in any instantaneous way. But there is an ultimate connection in that the state of all particles in the universe is infinitesimally affected by your every choice."

I remembered something else. "But he also said something about time. What was that all about?"

He waved his hand at me, trying to slow me down. "There will be more about that later. But here's something to think about: If the cloud of *Existence* starts at the point of origin and then spreads out into lower and lower probabilities, and if life often chooses the less probable, which direction is everything actually going within the cloud?"

"Well, I guess it's always moving from the cloud's middle toward the outer edges and toward lower probabilities," I answered. Then I laughed. "Another way of saying that is what people are always saying: life just keeps getting crazier and crazier."

"Exactly!" The critic laughed with me. "But there's a lot more to it than that."

He jumped off the chair and came toward me. "Are you ready for more?"

"I certainly am," I responded, and we folded.

16

Identity, Perception, and Qualia

(THE CRITIC'S NARRATIVE)

THE ARTIST WAS STILL speaking.

"However, some creatures can do more than use their senses to interact with their immediate environment: they can assemble the information from those senses into an overall sense of relationship—they have perception. You, too, will experience this when you enter *Existence*."

"I am looking forward to that," I muttered. "Right now, this all seems too alien to comprehend."

"Patience." The Artist smiled. "This will all make sense to you when you experience my work. But there is one more level to all of this. Some creatures—humans especially—have the advanced ability not only to perceive their own relationship to their environment but to extrapolate the relationships of other creatures to their relative environments as well, and even to imagine, with varying degrees of accuracy, the actual perceptions of those other creatures. In doing so, they can distinguish between themselves and other creatures, just as you and I can distinguish our relative experiences from each other's. They call this distinction 'identity.'

"They can also sense the probabilities of the next moment and choose the less probable path if they desire to do so. Most of the time, they move along the paths of greatest probability, but they also often deviate, creating a reality that becomes less and less probable and is always moving farther and farther away from the point of origin.

"The highest creatures among them—the focus of my work, humans—can also enter a relationship with me and can choose either to do so or to turn away from me. This, together with the sum of their ability to make choices in interacting with their environment, is what most of them call 'free will' but is more accurately labeled 'choice.'

"Thus, I created a setting in which my creatures not only perceive their environment as individuals but can also make choices that affect that environment. Since every creature has a different perspective, their perceptions create a myriad of overlapping realities." He paused, then turned to me. "What gives it even greater depth and makes it striking is how those perceptions internal to *Existence* can play off each other, creating incredibly complex veins and threads that make the overall creation much richer than my earlier work with *Heaven* and the angels.

"These less probable disruptions allowed for the development of a canvas on which I could portray—well, wildness. The tension between the various polarities was now tremendous, creating its own universe of probabilities, yet always defined by its distance from its point of origin, its own destruction. With that as a setting, I could create stories and experiences that would enable me—and you, and others—to see Eternity in a new light. *Existence*, with all of its themes of endings, is a direct contrast to Eternity.

"However, even life itself did not give me the sense of *experience* that I was seeking. I needed something else that would give direction to it all.

"That something was another force even greater than the mathematical forces of probability. This force is shared by those of us who inhabit Eternity, and it is not describable in mathematical terms, which is why my creatures' science will always fall short of a complete explanation for their existence. Some of their philosopher-scientists have called it 'qualia'—the qualities of the inner experience beyond what can be described by physics or biology, such as any individual experience of life. What they experience as beauty is far greater than the sum of light waves or the chemicals involved in pleasure. One's quale is one's actual experience of physical properties, not just the physical properties themselves.

"Qualia, together with the ability to make choices, distinguishes life from non-life."

He saw the confusion on my face. He spread his hands and explained, "Qualia is the act of observing something, or more accurately, experiencing something. In physics, it is what collapses a probability wave into an observable, fixed particle. We here in Eternity have experience. Qualia is *their* experience.

"Qualia, therefore, is what brings probability into reality. When a particle is unobserved, it exists as a wave functioning under the uncertainty principle: we cannot predict with certainty both its position and velocity at the same time. When it is observed, the wave breaks down, and we have a particle fixed in time and space—and memory. While we in Eternity have all of our experiences immediately available to us, humans and other creatures can only access experiences in their past through memory.

"Humans, for example, can see everything in relation to themselves, and their experience fixes everything's position in the past. They carry the memory of their reality into their future. The parts of their brains that store memories are translating experience as you or I know it into the physical reality of *Existence*. That is why, given physical limitations, they only remember so much in *Existence*—but when they come eventually to Eternity, they will recall everything, because here no such limitations exist."

The last word was delivered with an ironic smile and a raised eyebrow. I got it, and I nodded in return.

17

Qualia and the Arrow of Time

As I pulled away from the critic, I knew in some way that I was doing it much too often. I could feel his exasperation at my constant interruption. However, I was still human—obviously very limited, based on what the Artist was saying—and I could only take so much before I had too many questions to continue.

"Huh?" I asked in my most intellectual tone.

He snorted, maybe a little derisively. "Could you be a little more specific?"

I rallied a little. "I'm not getting it. What 'direction' was it that he needed, and what does this 'qualia' have to do with it?"

He smiled, and I was a little surprised to see patience in his expression.

"Let me take you back a little. You understand that the first three dimensions create physical space, right?"

"Right, that's basic," I replied.

"And then there is one more dimension basic to all three of those—time," he continued.

"Yes, I know."

"But what makes time go?"

At that point, I could barely comprehend the question. What makes time go? Well, time is . . . time. "Time doesn't go anywhere.

It just is what it is." Even as I said that, I realized what he was getting at. "Oh, you mean, what makes time move forward?"

"Yes!" I could see that he was relieved to have me back on track. "The quale is what drives time. You experience time as always moving forward into your future, never into the past." I nodded. "Well, that 'arrow of time' is actually further movement away from the point of origin through probabilities—probabilities that include new configurations of matter, energy, and space."

He waved his hand to stop my imminent question. "Imagine your own experience as a line—a type of dimension—and then include the element of qualia that is choice. Every moment of your experience generates probabilities made up of potential choices you could have made—timelines extending away from the line of your experience. Points along these probabilities intersect those of other creatures of choice, creating a dizzying array of shared probabilities."

"Just like the Venn diagram I mentioned earlier," I interjected.

"Right. But when you choose from among the probabilities, you perceive the choice you make, changing it from probability to reality. Your choices reverberate off the choices made by other living creatures, first within your vicinity and then beyond, and the final consequences of all those choices are made manifest by the reactions of the physical world around you. It's as if every choice you make is akin to a marble in a pinball machine, bouncing off the choices of others until a final net result comes into existence. And this is all happening at every moment in time. Your experience of that moment becomes part of your quale, and you are carried forward in time by that moment becoming part of your memory.

"Time moves only forward because it is formed by the construction of reality, which consists only of the established past—the combined observations by life and the overlapping experiences, the qualia, of that resulting reality—and the present, the current context of choosing from among probabilities. The future has no reality because the final choices cannot be made until the circumstances leading to that future become reality."

I must have looked confused, because he paused and then explained in a softer tone, "Imagine a moment in time. As you take a step forward, other life forms simultaneously make their moves, and from among all the probabilities of that instant, a moment of reality is rendered into existence. Immediately it becomes part of your experience, part of your short-term memory, and therefore cannot be experienced again. You are now a step *beyond* whatever choices you could have made in that previous moment. You have therefore moved forward in time.

"In a lifeless universe, time has no such direction because there is no reality—only probabilities. Time in such a context moves equally both forward and backward.

"You probably don't think of your choices as being mathematics," he said, and I nodded. "However, the instinct with which you make choices does not require you to do the mathematics consciously, any more than a boy throwing a ball into the air must calculate its trajectory before he catches it. Your very existence is a flow of the language of mathematics, and you move within that flow."

He raised a finger. "However, the extent of your quale—your experience of your choice—is limited. It does not include the qualia of other humans, or even the qualia of animals, plants, or bacteria. The mix of all these qualia usually results in the most probable being chosen—*most* of the time. However, as you already know, living creatures are not always predictable. What you expect to happen in the next moment is not always what happens, because it is driven by the sum of the choices of all life, instantaneously."

He pulled himself back into his chair and settled into his professorial demeanor.

"Let's say you're driving your car down the street toward home. All at once, for no reason at all, you suddenly make a U-turn, causing other people in the vicinity to stop and look at you for a moment. You still need to go home, so you round the block and get back on course.

"You have interrupted the flow of activity among the people who saw you make the turn, and their lives will be affected. They may arrive at their own destinations a second or two later, and you of course will arrive home a little later than would otherwise have been the case.

"However, like when a pebble is tossed into a pond, the ripple effects of your improbable choice to make the U-turn will most often die out, and what happens in the next hour, day, week, or month will eventually become what it would have become anyway.

"But who knows? Maybe your sudden move causes someone to step off a curb an instant later than he would have otherwise, and so he doesn't get hit by a truck. Or your later arrival at home means you never interact with your wife before she leaves for the store, and so all kinds of things change. In any of these cases, overall reality has veered in a more improbable direction, and all new possibilities emanate from that less probable reality."

"Okay, I understand that," I replied. "We talked about that earlier, when I said that life just keeps getting crazier. But what does that have to do with the arrow of time?"

"Well, qualia are also limited by the reverse attraction of the most probable and the improbable." He saw that didn't clarify anything for me, so he slowed down a little. "A 'moment' consists of not only the current configuration of matter and energy but also that configuration at that point in time. 'Now' has a current probability of 100 percent." I nodded. He continued, "The next moment has a probability of less than 100 percent; the choices of different people or other life could lead them in different directions. However, the moment with the highest probability has the strongest attraction, meaning it has the strongest 'pull' because all moments are attracted back along their dimensional lines to the zero of Eternity. The present moment stands between the next moment and the point of origin.

"That is why your U-turn will probably have little impact on the most probable reality most of the time. Since the force of the pull from the point of origin will follow a straight line to the current moment of probability, the strongest pull for the next point will come from the one of highest probability. That is why new universes of probability are not necessarily formed every time a particle moves. Even if its movement is one of low probability, the overall direction of reality will usually not be affected." He could see that I was following his explanation.

"Thus, you are pulled by probability to the future of greatest probability, but life nevertheless represents the ability to resist that pull and choose its next moment from those of lesser probabilities—just like your sudden decision to make the U-turn—and those choices *can* change the future to one of lesser probability. As noted before, however, once that future of lesser probability becomes reality, the future of greatest probability will change and now emanate from that new reality.

"So, one of the most interesting features of *Existence* is that, because of life, the overall qualia expand from greater to lesser probabilities. Just as you always expected, the experience of life becomes increasingly improbable—'crazier,' as you put it. Without life, *Existence* includes the probabilities that could have been completely and mathematically predictable, with only slight variations resulting from the uncertainty principle. However, the experience of living things—qualia—does not follow that path of probability."

He pointed to the cloud. "Just like you noted earlier, life keeps things moving farther away from the point of origin toward the edge of the cloud. Somewhere just within that cloud is a tiny point representing the end of the line for your reality. That point connects with the center of the cloud in a very crooked and winding line. That line is your arrow of time."

Suddenly, I got it. "And if something that's alive makes a less probable choice that affects the overall reality—like the person stepping off the curb a moment later and not getting hit by a truck—then the next point is off that original line, and a new line is formed."

"Almost," he answered, with a small smile. "Your explanation makes it sound like the line is straight leading back to the point of origin, but that would literally change your past. No, the *attraction* back to the point of origin follows a straight line, but the actual line of reality is anything but straight."

I laughed a little at the mental image, reality as a crooked line leading to the improbable, the unexpected. The old saying that the future is unpredictable was an understatement.

He continued, "But that is why the cloud has no definitive outer edge, no discernible shape. It's always getting bigger as your reality gets longer because every point of your reality generates more probabilities. The main body of the cloud has definition because the choices of the past—and therefore the alternative probabilities of the past—are permanently defined, but the outermost edge of the cloud—all the way around—represents all of the still unresolved probabilities generated by the most current moment of actual reality."

I had a sudden thought. "Wait, so an earthworm could make a choice that redirects the fate of the universe?"

He laughed.

"You humans have an old question that can be answered here: If a tree falls in a forest and there is no one to hear it, does it make a sound? Assuming that 'no one' refers to the complete nonexistence of life, and therefore of qualia, the answer is—no. There is nothing to interpret the waves produced by that event into sound—there is nothing with senses and perception to 'hear' it.

"You have many scientists and philosophers who cling to the idea of an objective reality, that your universe must exist independently of anyone's ability to perceive it—but that is nonsense. All around you in your world is the evidence that perception defines reality; the mistake is to assume that *human* perception is all that counts."

He chuckled. "Some of you who call yourselves 'creationists' argue that dinosaur fossils could have been created as already part of the earth, without the dinosaurs even having existed or walked the earth. They are right—if that were indeed the case, you humans would never know, because all that exists is your perception of the bones and your scientists' interpretation of what the bones mean."

He shrugged. "The dinosaurs might object to that—but their qualia don't directly intersect with you humans, so the final judge of that argument may be the crocodile."

He was waiting for me to laugh, but I was too distracted.

"So even the falling tree can change reality?"

He sighed, obviously disappointed in my lack of humor. "All life can make choices. Memory, perception, and identity, however, contribute to the impact of those choices. An earthworm in a normal situation is going to make highly probable choices. Those choices might determine whether it is crushed by the falling tree, and the tree itself never had the range of choices that even the earthworm has—but the tree and the earthworm are not interesting in themselves. The earthworm is highly unlikely to influence the overall qualia of all the life in its context, so the most probable future prevails.

"However, if the tree falls on something consequential, so that the ripples don't die out but rather result in new possibilities, then the seemingly inconsequential earlier choices in growing roots and branches—a root growing left instead of right when it encounters a rock straight on, for example—can have major impact.

"But who wants to watch a tree grow?" He shook his head and peered at me.

"You must understand how fascinating human qualia are to those of us in Eternity. Every experience, every moment throughout your history represents experience beyond our own, rich and illuminating. As I noted before, experience is what propels us through sequence in Eternity—and what the Artist created has given us experience beyond what we could have imagined.

"For, beginning with the split in Eternity, the Artist introduced the concept of *termination*. If the positive point is *here*, and thus the negative point is *there*, then the segment between them represents a 'finity.' And then, by translating qualia into *life*—which is anything but eternal—the Artist gave us a completely new perception of experience."

I recalled the Artist's reference to "stories" and had a sudden flash of anger. "So, what, we're just entertainment?"

"No, you are much more than that. And you already know that because you have your Bible, and the promises from your God are spelled out in there. The Artist even referred to your ability to form a relationship with him. But we're getting ahead of ourselves. Let's return to the Artist's story."

I wasn't ready yet. Looking at the cloud, I murmured, "So the current moment of my life is on the outer edge of that cloud, right?" I was intrigued, peering more closely at the grayish yet multicolored blob.

He laughed. "No, it's somewhere in the interior. The whole length of your life, from beginning to end, is completely contained in there. You're looking at all of existence, including time itself."

"What?" I was stunned at the implications. "So everything is already decided? I thought you said I had choices. If it's all in there already, isn't that predestination?"

"No, not at all," he responded, waving a finger. "Keep in mind that cloud is *all* the choices that could be made, by you or anything else. True, from this perspective you've already made them all, but at one time your choices were at the outer edge."

"No, what you're seeing now is the finished product. You're seeing all of *Existence*—including how it ends."

I gasped. "So, that's the future? Of everything?"

"Yes," he said, "but you can't *see* anything, any details. You'd have to stick your head into it to see those, and of course you can't do that on your own right now. But maybe now"—he smiled sagely—"you understand how the Artist can know everything, see everything, be everywhere, and yet give you choice."

I did. But to be standing there, looking at everything that ever could, did, would, *will* exist . . .

"Ready to return?" he asked, and I nodded, still a little numb. This time I didn't even see him coming, but suddenly we were folded again.

18

A Multiverse of Probability

THE ARTIST MADE A little flourish with his hand. "And that is why I call this my masterpiece. When you see it, you will never again see Eternity the same way as you do now. You will see the possibility of contrast in the growth of your own experiences—perhaps treasuring that growth even more than you do now. Such revelations are the purpose of art, and this work is more comprehensive in that respect than anything I have created before."

I stared at him, all his explanations coming together in my head in one staggering revelation. "I am still struggling to understand the basic concept of what you have described. You have found a way to make Eternity *end*?"

"No, not really," replied the Artist. "Eternity is still the source of the cloud, so in a sense the cloud is simply a distortion of Eternity. But by creating dimensions in relation to Eternity, I defined limitations through a range of distance from it. That range constitutes *Existence*, and its realities are defined by perceptions occurring at any point within it.

"However, there comes a point when all of life in every probability ceases to exist. At that point, only the uncertainty principle exists to grow the cloud. That is what you now see, a cloud that has basically finished growing but is still enveloped in that undefined outer layer of probability that fluctuates with the uncertainty principle." He gestured at the cloud's edges. "There is nothing to observe the particle's position, and so the outside is all fluctuating probability."

He turned back to me. "But inside, reality has been defined along a path, and much has begun and ended. So no, Eternity has not ended in any way, but in *Existence*, every universe ends."

I held a finger up. "You referred before to the term 'universe.' What do you mean by it?"

The Artist pointed to the cloud. "Universes are what especially lend to the lumpiness and asymmetries of the cloud. A universe is the sum of all related probabilities. When a choice is made, that shifts the overall direction of the greatest probabilities, and a new universe is created—made up of all the probabilities that emanate from that choice right up to the moment that the universe dies. At that moment there is no more potential for shifts in greatest probabilities."

Once again, I conveyed nothing but confusion.

"Okay." He drew a breath. "Let's assume something significant happens, say, a person who will one day become a leader and start a war makes a bad choice and instead is killed. Until that moment, the greatest probabilities reflected all the things that would happen leading up to the war and the consequences that followed from that war. However, the moment that person is killed, the war is no longer the greatest probability. There is a shift in probability—maybe now all the greatest probabilities reflect that person's sibling becoming the leader and creating alliances that end the prospect of war.

"The first set of probabilities is one universe, and the second set is a second universe. Perhaps the first universe's probabilities extend further from the eternal point of origin than the second universe's—the first universe lasts longer, in other words. So, the first universe produces more of a bump on the outside of the cloud, while the second is more of an indentation."

"I think I understand," I replied, "although I'm not sure I like the idea of 'war' and other terms you used. But I assume I'll be finding out soon." I glanced at the cloud.

"I look forward to your reaction." The Artist smiled. "But let me continue.

"So, I end up with an incredible variety of possible universes, each differing from the other by only a few degrees. And in every one of those universes, there are physical properties and laws that account for every aspect of its existence, including the universe's own history of how it came into being.

"And, as I noted before, life is what chooses the realities. It is life that predominantly captures the moment, collapses the wave function of probability into actual particles, and often chooses the less probable over the more probable. When those choices lead to shifts in the overall greatest arc of probabilities, a new universe is born. However, only one of those universes is rendered reality; the others all remain probabilities. As those other universes are left behind, however, they nonetheless remain mathematically accessible when probabilities are calculated or traced.

"But none of those other universes really matter. Just as when you look at a sculptured statue, you care only about the artistry and impact of its exterior and do not care at all about what supports it from inside, so too do you regard my own work. It doesn't really matter what lies behind it. My creatures have chosen their universe from the multiverse. Theirs is not the most perfect or stable universe but rather the one that contains just the right amount of—wrongness, chaos, adversity, or whatever you want to call it—to create the drama for which I was searching and to which they have brought themselves.

"That section of *Existence* contains the creatures who are the focus of my work. While the creatures are part of the cloud, they have the perception of moving through it; they see particles or matter only in sequence rather than all at once, and they remember, to varying degrees of accuracy, how they came to the present. As I've mentioned before, they call this perception 'time.'

"You may recognize it as closely resembling the experience of sequence. Each creature's perception of its experience differs from the perceptions of others, but together they direct themselves through a specific range of the dimensions of probability. Ironically, even though the entire cloud is here in *Existence*, my creatures experience only the tiniest fraction of it—actually, only a plane—from one point to another; that is what I was referring to when I mentioned their 'present.' And while they can remember what they experienced earlier in their perceived sequences, they are unable to see what will be coming up next."

I was struggling to comprehend all of this, but then his last statement sank in. "You made them blind?" I asked incredulously. I could only imagine these creatures groping along a path shadowed on both sides and always facing a wall of blackness.

"Oh, it's even tougher than that. Their perceptions are limited only to the immediately available probabilities, and therefore to only a small portion of the cloud. From their perspective, their existence is even further limited to what they perceive as their beginnings—'birth'—to an ending they cannot avoid, called 'death.'"

"Then what is the point of such a state?" I demanded. "From what you describe, I can imagine your creatures in complete despair; after all, not only is their universe limited in duration but their experience within it has its own short length. Their experiences, their 'lives,' appear almost completely meaningless, without purpose or effect."

"But that is also the source of their nobility!" he cried. "Even given those limitations, they are willing to sacrifice their experiences, their very lives, to have a relationship with me, their creator!"

"Fascinating," I murmured, not convinced. "But then, you created them to want that relationship, right? They're not really in control of that."

"Wrong," responded the Artist triumphantly. "They *are* in control of that! I simply gave them the ability to choose between the planes of their own existence or the Eternity of their creator. But it's more than that, much more."

"What?" I asked. "How is it more? What is this whole thing really about?"

"Imagine," replied the Artist, "that a creature could desire the company of another—could desire to give up its own identity to be unified with another—even when achieving that goal would mean incredible pain, or would require overcoming impossible obstacles.

"*Then* imagine that those same creatures might also desire a relationship with their creator, even be willing to give up their lives for the chance to share Eternity with me. Imagine that they would be able to overcome doubt and fear to welcome me into their limited time in *Existence*, even though they are unable to fully see me. Imagine that the fact of their existence is proof enough for them to believe in and desire a relationship with their creator.

"That is the primary feature of *Existence*. It is a work within a work.

"I call this work 'Love.'"

He put his hand on my shoulder and nodded toward the cloud. Together, the Artist and I leaned and inserted our heads into the cloud.

Perception

I AM.

I know I am because I can see, I can smell, I can taste, I can hear, and I can touch. I sense my organic boundaries and internal processes, and I feel the proximity and motion of what is around me.

My senses reach out and arrest particles undefined in motion. Before I sense them, they lack reality—but when I sense them, they are there.

Even as I am here because I am sensed.

It is not just that the leaf I caress between my fingers exists because I touch it. I am here because the leaf was touched by my hand.

Does the world behind me exist? The tree's roots reach beneath my feet in a universe of microbes, insects, and the roots of other plants. Those roots in turn reach out to be brushed against by creatures that choose their own pathways through the complexity of life and the passivity of insensate earth.

I am surrounded by perception, and perception forms my state of being. The moon hangs in the sky as a product of physical forces that were not only perceived by those who have observed mindlessly but also interpreted by those who ever seek to analyze and understand.

The mouse did not hang the moon, but the moon hangs in some small part because the mouse is there to see it.

Life defines reality. Without life, there would be no definition. There would be no perception. There would be no me.

And I am.

19

A Bit of Confusion

Suddenly, the critic and I were back in the studio.

"How was it for you?" he asked, obviously curious.

I shook my head. "I'm not quite sure what just happened. I was just me, although I'm not quite sure where I was in my life. It was as if I was inside my whole life looking out, but I didn't really have a chance to absorb any of it."

He frowned. "Oh, that wasn't what I expected. I thought you would experience what I experienced."

I was surprised by his confusion. "So you and the Artist weren't really looking at my life?"

"Not at all," he responded, staring into the distance. "I was seeing all the incredible stories of people throughout *Existence*. I wonder . . . but no, that can't work."

He looked at me with his brow furrowed. "If you don't see what I see when I look in the cloud, you're not going to understand what's going on." He looked as if he were blaming me somehow.

Then I got it. He *was* blaming me!

"Look, I know I wrote it, but right now, I don't know any more than you do," I retorted.

He shook his head and waved his hands. "Never mind, never mind, I'm sure it all works out. After all, I barely experienced anything that time myself. I was overwhelmed by the sense of relationship between the Artist and—oh!" He brightened and smiled. "You're not one of us, so you can't sense any of that. You can't feel the Artist and the connection to his work."

He saw my puzzlement and smiled encouragingly. "Never mind, you'll see what I mean. Let's go back."

I shrugged, stepped forward, and we folded again.

20

Love

ALMOST IMMEDIATELY, I WITHDREW from the cloud, gasping. The Artist turned to me, smiling, and waited.

I shook my head to clear it. "I felt as if I had penetrated to your very heart. Everything in that cloud, it's you!"

"Precisely," answered the Artist.

"But the perceptions, the experiences, the sheer brevity of it"—I looked around the studio, my voice strangling away—"it makes Eternity look . . . *vast* . . . and different."

"Isn't that the purpose of art?" asked the Artist, smiling with pleasure.

"You're right. This is a masterpiece. May I . . . *can* I look again?"

"By all means, go ahead! But I should tell you that there is a difference between what you and I are experiencing."

"What is that difference?" I asked.

"When I insert myself into the cloud, it all becomes a part of me. It's integrated through me, and I remain in it even when I pull back into Eternity. It exists because I will it to exist; I made the choice to split the particle. When *you* insert yourself, it moves aside and around you to allow you to view it, but it's not part of you. The eternity that is you cannot mix with it, and its probabilities do not include you. To *Existence*, I am the one and only Creator; everything depends upon *my* willing it to exist. You are only a spectator."

"But what a spectacle!" I gushed. In my excitement, I had lost all pretense of dignity. "The range of stories, the multiple—what did you call them? Perceptions! How is it that I can see the same thing in so many ways, often even in contradictory ways? And what is that sense of desire that haunts everything I see?"

"You are experiencing love," replied the Artist. "That is the element of tone throughout this work. The creatures in this work call it 'emotion,' but all emotions in fact stem in one way or another from that one basic emotion, love.

"Love is a desire for connection to something greater than oneself. It replicates to a degree our own desire for experience with a yearning for meaning and fulfillment. Ultimately, my intention was for my creations to seek me through love, and to find me both through faith in me and through love for each other. In fact, my own union with each of them is represented in the act of mating, where two of them unite, become one with each other, and then populate their world with their offspring, who then repeat the cycle.

"But because I gave them choice and the power to manipulate their world, some choose other objects of love, what I have described to humans as 'false gods.' Love then takes the form of greed, selfishness, envy, frustration, or even the very denial of love, which they call 'hatred.' They can experience the effects of connection through love with me or each other, which they call 'joy.' They can channel their love into service to others or distort that very outlet into a hunger for power—the desire to be served and to control. They can even sink into a despair that is the effect of the desire to be loved, the need for validation and meaning to be bestowed upon them by others, never realizing that their desperation to receive it prevents them from giving it and then, in turn, getting it."

"But why all the pain? Why the tragedy, the grief, the sheer horror that I saw?" I was still shaking. "Doesn't it seem to you that you are being unspeakably cruel to them?"

"You were in there for only an abbreviated experience, and you have not yet taken in the overall story. You were bombarded with everything at once," answered the Artist in a gentle tone. "Even though you sensed everything as an extension of me, you did not yet take on the perception of me that the creatures have in common.

"You asked me before about the element of perception. Each creature is immersed in a constant reality; they are all part of the cloud, and every point of their being is entangled with another part of *Existence* and then, of course, they are entangled with each other, to greater or lesser degrees depending upon the probabilities of their location in time and space. Yet they are aware of distance and other features of contrast, and they experience identities that are unique in *Existence*. First, every creature is born with a unique structure; then, as their awareness emerges into their personal part of *Existence*—their lives—they experience their interactions with the rest of *Existence*—their qualia—and how they interact is a function of their freedom of choice.

"But the same is true for how other creatures react to those choices of interaction—no one can control the outcome of their choices, only the choice itself. So, one person chooses to act in a certain way, and another reacts to that action—but both people view the action and reaction through the color of their own experiences and desires. Thus, they can have completely different perceptions of what just took place."

"You haven't answered my question, though," I interrupted. "Not all the pain that I just saw is the direct result of the victims' choices. I saw tragedies beyond their control—times when the wind or the seas or the skies themselves unleashed horrors upon them. Why do you let those things happen?"

The Artist sighed. "Those events are a feature of the chaos that comes from the instability of their universe—the uncertainties of particles and the laws of physics—as well as their own cumulative venture into greater improbabilities. But that is not what is truly important.

"They do not understand that they are, in fact, eternal beings." He nodded toward the cloud. "They know it—they've been instructed both by me and by others speaking with my voice that this is true, but they cannot grasp it within their own limited experience of *Existence*. Just as you now see Eternity with different eyes by experiencing *Existence*, so too will they see Eternity, though they will do so from the limited perspective of *Existence*.

"However, the very nobility of these creatures is breathtaking! You, my friend, have never been faced with the prospect of losing yourself, of ending. Not only have they faced that in every moment of their lives but some among them have also chosen to sacrifice their lives—either completely, as have soldiers or other heroic individuals, or in vast stretches through service or dedication to others without reward."

He flung his arms wide at the cloud. "The world they know places them in peril all the time. They cannot escape the threat of death, and they constantly witness the despair of others who have lost what they love. And yet, despite all these things, even though they do not directly see me, their creator, they nevertheless accept the significance of their very existence as the proof that I am, and they place their faith in those proofs and choose to love me as well.

"That is what I made them to do, but I gave them the *choice* to do it. And out of that choice comes all the epic results of love—nobility, heroism, selflessness, perseverance, and yes, tragedy, sacrifice, and grief."

He saw my lips purse and smiled. "But is it cruel? You know better than that, but you're still grappling with the fact that they are one with me, and I am one with them. If they were limited to *Existence*, then I could not face your judgment with anything but shame.

"But they will know Eternity, and then what they have experienced in their existence—even though it will have shaped their very beings and will eternally define their perceptions—all of that will be but the passing of a moment. Without the struggle, there would be no stories—nor would there be courage, determination, nobility, selflessness, nor victory. But even more important, they would not have the experience that allows them subsequently to make the right decisions in Eternity.

"Those who choose my will, who seek a relationship with me, will be rewarded with their own names—the word that defines each of them and brings them into existence—and then they will no longer have to fear for their existence because they will be able to speak it for themselves."

"I am amazed," I murmured. "This work is layers upon layers, and yet it is also fundamentally simple." I turned to him, my eyes brimming, my mind swirling, and my heart overflowing with what I had just experienced in only the equivalent of a glance. Timidly, I asked, "Do you mind? May we return?"

"Of course!" exclaimed the Artist, and together we again inserted ourselves into the cloud.

Struggle

BREATHS THAT SEEM TO *burst from chaos. The swirl of her mind as she lunges through the tunnel of green. The heat of her infant's fever burning into her arms and breast even in the oppressive oven of the jungle. She can think of only the safety of the clinic, the kindness of the strange people who will help her baby.*

She falls, twisting her body instinctively to protect her oddly quiet child. The crack of her rib, the wrenching pain exploding through her chest erase for a moment even her infant from her mind. There is only red, black, fire and pinwheels of light—but then, as the wave subsides, she opens her eyes to the green canopy above her. Beneath her back, the wetness of the hole into which she has stumbled. Her baby! The thought makes her wrench upward, and pain collapses everything.

When the whirlpool fades and her eyes finally see, she is already running again. She glances down at her child, and he is still there, apparently unharmed but still consumed within his own silent inferno. Every step jars her broken rib. Agony cries out for her both to stop and to keep going. She runs, runs, and runs.

At first, she is not even aware of the bite. But she falls yet again, this time twisting away from the baby's side, the impact of the earth blowing her breath completely from her lungs. Now another fire, spreading up from her ankle through her leg, a cold, hostile numbness in its wake. Instantly she associates the pain with snakebite, the creep of fatal poison. But no, her child! Her mind is screaming, and then she is moving yet again, stumbling, somehow placing weight on a leg that seems to be missing, the sharp cracks of agony from her rib now perversely serving to keep her conscious and alert.

And then she stops, air whistling wetly through her swollen, arid lips, every instinct alert. The cat crouches before her, tail whipping from side to side, eyes glowing. Carefully, slowly, she lowers herself to the ground, free arm scrabbling in the grass and dirt, clawing, grabbing. She sees the muscles tense as the cat prepares to spring—and suddenly her hand whips forward, dirt and rocks slapping the cat's eyes. It springs not forward but sideways, shaking its head, pawing at its eyes, and she is running again, running again, running again.

She slams into a yielding hardness and hears the intake of breath and cry of the woman as if the sounds were in slow motion. She is seeing the woman, her oddly pale skin, her brown eyes, her strange clothing, and the baby in the woman's arms as she slips down, down, down.

21

The Reason

I WAS STUNNED. I was not even aware of my disengagement from the critic.

I had just been another person, and for that matter, a woman. I had felt what she felt, thought what she thought, suffered what she suffered—and died her death. All without any sense of my own identity. One moment I had been me, the next her, and now, here I was again.

I felt a hand on my shoulder and turned to see the critic peering up into my face. "What is happening?" he asked. Where there should have been an expression of concern on his face, I saw instead an intense curiosity. Where there should have been humanity, I saw only—interest.

All at once, a hot rage slammed into me. I put my hands on his chest and pushed, hard, stepping back from him.

"What is happening?" I screamed back at him. "That's exactly what I want to know! That woman. She died! She went through hell and she died and her child won't know her! And she did *nothing* to deserve it—any of it!"

I spun around to face the cloud, then turned back to him, my arms outstretched, my insides convulsing. "Entertainment! All of this, everything, it's all just for you to experience, to be . . . *entertained*?"

The critic remained silent, but he shifted his gaze to the cloud instead of me. I stood there, breathing hard, my mind exploding with fury and the need to strike out, to break something, someone.

There was still no real sense of time. We stood in those positions as my anger slowly faded. The shrieking in my head and the thrumming of my veins all gradually died down. Finally, I spoke, a ragged whisper: "Is that all we are?"

The critic returned his gaze to me. Softly, with a tenderness that had not been there before, he replied, "You *are* the Artist."

He began to walk toward me, slowly, one step at a time. "You are his masterpiece. You are his love. You are the reason for everything." He paused, looked down, then gazed at me, actual pleading in his expression. "*Everything.*" He took one step closer, then stopped. "You are the reason he *died.*"

I looked down, and the entire experience—the woman, this studio, my own life—crashed in on me at once. I began to sob silently, I felt the critic's arm encircle my shoulders, and we folded.

22

Poignancy and Pain

(THE CRITIC'S NARRATIVE)

As WE EMERGED FROM the cloud, tears brimmed over and streamed down my cheeks. "I am speechless," I whispered, staring intently at the cloud. The Artist stood near, silent. "I saw a woman carrying her sick infant through the jungle. She fell and broke a rib, she was bitten by a snake, she fought off attacks by predators, and she still managed to reach a clinic. She died even as she delivered her baby into the nurse's arms. She endured so much, had no idea that there would ever be anything more, and yet she was willing to give up her very *existence* for her child!" I shook my head, and more tears rolled down my cheeks. "I have never seen such incredible stories, one atop another, trillions of them!"

"And all of them are about one thing: love," murmured the Artist, smiling.

"Yes, but that story includes horrors too, such that I have never before imagined! They call it 'evil,' and many of them believe you are perfectly 'good.' I found this to be perplexing." I wiped my face and turned to face the Artist. "You are their God."

"Yes, that is a complicated term," replied the Artist. He shook his head. "When I spoke to one of them, he asked me my name. I was at first affronted by the question—who was he to ask about my creation? But then I realized he simply wanted to be able to refer to me, as they do with the names they create for each other. I gave him a distinction between them and me—they were brought into existence, and I simply am. But they called me 'Yahweh'—oddly enough, a name that means it should not be spoken.

"They don't really grasp the concept of eternity," he marveled. "To them, it means time without end. At one point they finally come to understand the constraint of time to their own universe, but they are still unable to comprehend anything without it being part of their perceptions. Their scientists unravel existence with their formulae, yet even to them, eternity is just a never-ending form of time."

"And yet, through their existence, you have brought new meaning to how I see Eternity!" My enthusiasm was spilling over. "That they are restricted to a particular beginning and a particular end is devastating. But even given the brevity of their lives, they still choose to sacrifice it for others! All for this 'love' that you have created.

"Still," I said, my mood darkening, "it seems so purposeless, so futile."

"That is why I have given myself to them and ask that they give themselves to me," replied the Artist. "If all there was to their lives was what you see there, it would indeed be futile. But every one of them is my work. When I speak the words that define them—their true names—they are each of them unique among all others. If they choose to love me, then they will be one with me and will experience Eternity. I will let them help me shape my next work."

"But what if they bring their chaos and evil to your next work?" I cried, alarmed.

"They won't. They will be one with me, and the choices they make will be consistent with who I intended them to be and the roles I intended them to fulfill."

The Artist sighed and then explained, "At some point, all of them question my nature and intentions for them. The issues of death, suffering, and evil can overwhelm the experience of our relationship. They think of me as perfect—a rather ironic term, since their entire existence is subject to my will. The very definition of perfection comes from my creation. They cannot even fathom other possibilities or compare one perfection to another possible perfection—it is not within their grasp.

"But what I did give to them is the ability to discern what is consistent with my will—'perfect'—and what is not. It is this sense—some call it 'poignancy'—to which their own artists appeal with every work they create. Poignancy is the tension between the way they *know* things should be—perfection—and how it really is. It is the source of irony." He laughed suddenly, slapping his hands together. "Even the comic who walks across the stage and slips on the banana peel is appealing to their sense of irony and poignancy. In the perfect world, one wouldn't slip on a banana peel. The surprise, the tension between what they would normally expect to happen and what actually happens is what makes them laugh."

"But that is also what makes them cry," I responded. "Of all the pain and suffering you created, what affected me the most was when parents saw their children suffer and die."

"Yes," answered the Artist. "If they did not understand that a child should not die before the parent does, their pain would be much less. Their agonies are made sharper by their awareness that it is not how things should be.

"Still, they remain capable of choice. They may not be in control of their circumstances, but they are in control of how they respond to them. They maintain a sense of justice even as their universe displays a cold, unfeeling, and uncaring reality. That persistence in believing in justice defines the nobility of the human spirit.

"As I became a part of them, I allowed their pain to redefine me. I am looking forward to lifting every one of them from their former existence, drying every tear, and showing them the glories of Eternity so that the questions of their own existence become insignificant—even as that existence nevertheless helped to define them, as our own experiences continue to define us."

"Yes, that strikes me as especially imaginative," I said. "You made them, but then they are still the product of their own choices and life experiences." I smiled. "As with any great work of art, it is transformative."

The Artist grinned in delight, and gave a brief bow. "That is a mighty compliment coming from you! I appreciate your praise, but I do not want you to miss the even greater qualities of this work."

"You mean the idea of love? Don't worry, it's inescapable. There is just so much, such richness, that it is hard to take it all in," I said.

"Again, thank you, and I am very glad you also see the quality of love. It was very difficult to render, and I was constrained by my own rules: free choice, natural outcomes, and so on. I could have recreated those rules at any point, but the real effort of this piece comes from my own self-imposed limitations." The Artist laughed again. "My creatures' theologians have an old riddle: could God make a rock so heavy that he could not lift it? The answer was always so obvious—yes he could, and that rock was their freedom of choice!"

"But *did* pain and suffering have to be part of your creation?" I demanded. "Your creatures seem to struggle with the concepts of good and evil, and they never really seem to come to a final answer. I must say, I don't either. It's hard for me to see it from their perspective because it means so much to them, yet I don't even see what they are talking about.

"I mean, yes, I can see the evil of creatures taking upon themselves the decision to end the existence of others, of playing God. But they seem to see evil as a nature, not just as an event or act."

"That is because you are not subject to it," the Artist said gently. "They have made the issue into a great debate, and yet it is actually quite simple. If they choose to love me, then they want to follow my will because I am their Creator and they should want to fulfill what I intended for them. They can sense what is perfect and they should want to strive to achieve that. They can do it in any of a number of ways—all that I want is for them to use the unique gifts I incorporated into them—but they can also choose *not* to do so. When they choose to love me, that is good. When they choose to love me through loving others, that is also good. When they choose to love only themselves, that is evil. Simply put, evil is the result of them following their own desires instead of trying to discern mine for them."

(INTERLUDE)

Throughout this experience, I did not separate from the critic—oddly, I remained in the state of observing through the critic's eyes—his experience—yet I was aware of myself as distinct from him.

I understood that I could not at this point experience what he was experiencing. He had viewed *Existence* from a perspective similar to the Artist's. I could only view it as the human being I was—or, as in the case of the woman in the jungle, from the experience of another singular human being. The critic had obviously taken in many human experiences all at once.

He was experiencing enlightenment in his exposure to the human experience, whereas I was all too familiar with it already. As their conversation continued, I felt some frustration in feeling like an observer rather than directly participating in the critic's experience.

However, I was experiencing my own enlightenment. For the first time, I was beginning to see the Artist not just as a character interacting with the critic but as God—or, rather, God-ish. I still could not reconcile with the idea that I was seeing the Creator, the Almighty, or even Jesus Christ. I believe I was constrained through the experience of the critic, who—although openly admiring of the Artist—was nevertheless his peer. Still, I was beginning to appreciate, at least intellectually, the idea that I *was* looking at the very reason for my existence.

(THE CRITIC'S NARRATIVE)

"The question of pain and suffering is best answered in their example of Adam and Eve," the Artist continued. "Here are two people created to be in direct relationship with their creator. They are separated from the wildness and threats of the rest of the world and insulated within a garden that gives them everything they need. By knowing me face-to-face, they cannot claim not to know my will. Everything is perfect—none of the experiences of pain and suffering that other humans use to accuse God of injustice are present in their world.

"And yet Adam and Eve still choose to disobey their friend and creator. Their story illustrates that innocence and security are not compatible with freedom of choice, and like the angels, their fall is inevitable.

"But those who endure what they experience in their existence and nevertheless choose to pursue a relationship with me—they will be a different kind of creature when all is said and done. They will be my creations, but they will also have been shaped by their experiences. Once they join me in Eternity, they will have no inclination to choose to follow any desires but mine, because they have already experienced the lesser nature of a world shaped by the choice to defy me. That is how creatures with freedom of choice will nevertheless be one with me.

"What a relationship!" he suddenly exclaimed. "Even you will see me not just as another entity like yourself but as something shaped by everything you see in there." He nodded toward the cloud.

"In fact, I am already different." His expression became troubled and dark. "Unlike you, I have known the fact of existence. I have even died."

23

The Ultimate Sacrifice

(THE CRITIC'S NARRATIVE)

I WAS SPEECHLESS. I stared at the Artist, then held up my hands in confusion. "You died? You ended? How could you . . . wait, I don't see that in you. That is not part of your expression."

"You cannot see that in me until you see it through their eyes," the Artist said, gesturing toward the cloud. "They see me through their relationship with me, as the source of their existence. You do not. But when they become part of me, when I incorporate their experience into my own, you will then see it.

"That will be the ultimate expression of this work. It will become one with me, and all of its richness will become a part of the expression of my experience. Once you experience it all, you too will see it as part of me."

"But I don't understand how *you* could have ended, even in there!" I pointed at the cloud. "They *saw* you? I thought you made them dependent upon their faith in you. To expose yourself in that way violates the integrity of your work!"

"Once again, I used perception to shape how they interacted with me—but I also entered into my own limited perception so that I could become a part of their existence," explained the Artist.

"I was aware of them believing in a 'Jesus Christ,' and while that seemed to be related to belief in you, it made no sense to me," I murmured, gazing at the cloud.

"That is my name as one of them," replied the Artist. "You would be shocked to see me as they do. In fact, they will always see me that way. It is the face they know and will always know. To allow them to see more would change their very definition. They are the product of my word, my will. While they will someday control the fact of their existence, they will nevertheless remain my creation.

"But their perception of me is also that of one like them who sacrificed his existence for their sake. It will shock you even more when you finally see me that way—mutilated and even destroyed, yet restored. You will see those scars as part of my very definition."

"Why?" I whispered. "Was this"—I flung my arms out as if to embrace the cloud—"not enough?"

"No, it wasn't. Quite frankly, I was headed for failure. I made everything dependent upon their desire for Eternity but then, through *Existence*, prevented them from grasping Eternity. Like you, for them to truly see Eternity for what it was, they had to see it end—but even more important, they had to see it restored. They needed to see the link between their own existence and the promise of Eternity, or what they call 'immortality.'

"I tried so hard to show them the way, but always I knew that my efforts were not enough. They have a saying, 'Eat, drink, and be merry, for tomorrow we die,' which was the natural expression of the despair of existence.

"As their creator, I tried to overcome that, but the way they exercised their freedom of choice constantly exasperated me. They defied my will in every way."

"Wait a minute, you're losing me," I interrupted. "Tell me the story from the beginning."

"As with all art, it would be more effective to show you." The Artist chuckled. "Let's go back into the cloud and I'll guide you to understanding."

I nodded, and this time more eagerly bent into the cloud. Together, we regarded humans in their earliest discernible form.

"At first, I thought their sense of wonder at their own existence would lead them naturally to me," explained the Artist. "They hunted, found shelter, discovered fire, and loved and reproduced—but unlike the other creatures around them, they felt the need to thank someone for all of that.

"They were on the right track, but they reduced me to their own world. If the animal surrendered its life, they thanked it and then eventually turned it into a god of sorts. If something like lightning frightened them, then they attributed its power to godliness and worshipped it. I was frustrated; this was not what I wanted."

He then motioned to an area of reality. "So, I chose just a few and interacted with them directly." He shrugged. "Actually making myself known to them would, you would think, remove all doubts and possibly even their ability to choose. Still, they did have freedom of choice, and they did eventually turn away from me. It was my hope that, having known me, they would still choose to love me even after they failed to follow my will and experienced the harsher realities of existence—and they did.

"But their children had never known me directly, and their parents' stories were not enough to keep them faithful. Those children went on within the world, mixed with and mated with their wilder fellows, and descended once more into a hedonistic culture that reduced me to idols."

At this point, the Artist withdrew from the cloud, and I reluctantly followed him.

He sighed. "At one point I even threatened to destroy everything and start over. But there were always one or two or more I could point to who still loved me appropriately, who were able to grasp the fact of their existence and reach out to me on the basis of their own faith.

"So I decided to set aside a group of them. This group would then serve as a model for everyone else.

"It was at that point that I truly experienced the ups and downs of love and relationship." He sighed again. "I could turn the world upside-down for them, and in only a few short years they would cast some statue—often the representation of an animal—and worship it instead of me." He threw up his arms in despair. "It was an insult to me—but to change it would be to give up on my own creation. There had to be a way to give them an awareness of Eternity!"

"You sound like one of them, blundering around blind corners searching for inspiration," I commented. "Surely you knew the answer from the beginning."

"I did," replied the Artist. "But first I had to establish that there was no other way." He looked at me. "Would you have accepted my death as the answer if I had not first demonstrated the futility of the other strategies?"

"I would not have accepted your death at all, and I still don't," I replied sharply. "You are their Creator! Why must you be a victim of your own work?"

"Because to solve the problem as the Creator would have impugned my integrity," replied the Artist. "I knew starting out that there was only one way. If I were going to commit to this project as an artist, then I had to be prepared to subject myself to my own limitations.

"I had to enter into their own world and see it only as they could see it. I had to set an example, prove that it was possible to live a life in obedience to the Creator's will.

"And I had to die their death—cut off from my Creator—a death in which my only hope was based on my own faith. And then—finally—I had to show them that death is not the end, that death does not have the ultimate power.

"And, quite simply, that is what I did," murmured the Artist—and as his gaze met mine, I felt a chill.

Epiphany

SHE WAS ADRIFT IN a red haze, a cool mist left behind by the coarse sweat bursting through the agony of her effort. She was done, spent, yet her body shuddered and surged as if trying still to expel what had already been delivered.

But there was a voice, a faint tug through the fog, calling her name. "Mary, Mary." She opened her eyes to see the rough timbers of the stable roof above her and heard again the gentle protests of the sheep and cattle unaccustomed to sharing their home with humans in the night.

There, hovering above her, was the heavy face of the midwife, the stranger Joseph had found to help her through her ordeal. There, too, was the unreadable face of Joseph—dear, sweet Joseph, stoic to the end in a flood of events that he could not fathom but simply accepted.

And then there was warmth in her arms and against her bosom, and she heard the midwife's voice again: "It is a boy. You have a son."

Joseph slid his corded arm gingerly under her shoulders and lifted her, stuffing a blanket behind her head. And she looked down and saw, nestled in her arms, the child.

He lay there quietly, stained in red gore, yet with the sheen of the newly created. Then she looked into his eyes, and all at once she could not breathe.

For she was looking into the serene eyes of her own Maker. Even as she held him, streaked with her own blood, even as she cradled the child she carried and delivered, she held her own Father, her very designer.

And he was small and naked, unable to walk, to speak, to defend himself. His very mortal life was hers to take away in an instant, yet his eyes showed only peaceful trust.

For this, she had been born. The Lord of the thunder and the seas, the shaper of the winds and the stars, he who holds her eternity in his fingers like a speck of dust—he lay there, tiny and vulnerable, helpless, needing her.

Her parched lips broke apart, and she spoke softly. "His name is Jesus."

And she began to suckle him.

24

Eternity Made Mortal

I HAD JUST WITNESSED the first Christmas. That I had done so through the eyes of the critic was immaterial to me. I had seen the fact of it, not the myth.

The event bore little resemblance to the nativity scene so familiar to me in my lifetime. True, Joseph had been there, and the animals, but the midwife, the pain, the blood . . .

. . . and the baby. In the critic's perspective and therefore my own, he was framed not just within the stable but within the world, the universe. To call him vulnerable was a massive understatement. The forces of resistance confronted him. He breathed, but his lungs faced the same tensions all mortals face. His heart beat and his blood moved, yet there was friction that had to be overcome with strength. Every force that could end his life was arrayed in the reality that enveloped him.

The atoms that formed him had come from the earth. And he needed more of the earth to continue: the air that entered his lungs and permeated his bloodstream, the energy from the sun, trapped beneath the skies, that warmed him, and the human milk from a woman's breast that fed him and became part of him.

All the while, beside the critic, beside me, was this eternal Artist—next to me within the critic, yet also cradled before me in that all-too-human frame. I had witnessed Eternity made mortal.

(THE CRITIC'S NARRATIVE)

The Artist stood next to me, his arms crossed.

"So you became—finite," I murmured in astonishment.

"Indeed I did. It was the most amazing experience—have you ever heard of courage?" His sudden question surprised me.

"Courage . . . that is what the woman was demonstrating as she carried her infant through the jungle," I answered slowly, almost tasting the words passing through my lips as I relived the experience in my mind.

"Yes, right! It is the determination to proceed, to do what one believes to be right, even in the face of great harm or destruction. It is a by-product of love, although like everything else concerning love, it can be perverted. At any rate, I was thrilled to find that I had it. There were moments when I dreaded the end, the pain, everything that I knew would come, but I kept on going anyway.

"I didn't want to lose my sense of who I am, because I had to remain focused on my purpose for being among them. But oh, what I gave up!" he exclaimed, his eyes taking on a faraway look.

"Did you simply enter the world, or were you—born?" I asked, my eyes wide.

"Oh, I was born! I was actually conceived and developed as a fetus within a woman's womb, and I emerged into the world as any other infant. I had made certain in advance, using my angels, that my mother had a sense of who I was to be, because I was going to be vulnerable during my childhood.

"But there I was, an infant, with no knowledge of Eternity, of the world into which I'd been born, of language, of anything. My mother had freedom of choice and could have killed me even when the midwife placed me at her breast. But of course, I knew beforehand that wouldn't happen. It wasn't all perfect." He chuckled. "Once they even lost me for several days during a trip, when I was still a child.

"The relationship between my eternal self and my earthly self was akin to father and son, and as the Father, I could intervene lightly at different points to make certain my earthly self stayed on the right track—after all, I too had freedom of choice. But in my earthly form—as Jesus of Nazareth—I had little sense of what tomorrow would bring, of where the world was headed. I was still the Creator, so it was easy for me to look at people and *read* them, and I had an enhanced ability to select probabilities so that I could perform what others saw as miracles. This was all necessary so that those around me could make the association between the man before them and their own Creator.

"But it allowed me to live among them and teach them peer to peer. I cannot begin to describe to you the sense of wonder and fulfillment that comes from living a finite and precious life dedicated to a finite purpose! I was aware of Eternity, my identity as the Creator, and my destiny—and yet it was all based on faith rather than certainty. I experienced the doubt, the hesitancy, and the fear of losing my life or of failing in my purpose." At that, both of us fell silent, each pondering what it meant to exist in the face of nonexistence.

Finally, he spoke. "You have to see it to understand it, although even that will not be enough. Let me show you."

I nodded, and once again we entered the cloud.

Exegesis

Pain. Black. Buzzing, swirling. Voices whispering, screaming, dying away.

Fire in his wrists, his feet, around and within his head.

He struggled to open his eyes, and his lids broke free of the crusted blood and the salt of his sweat. The world was white, and it burned him.

Anguish rose up from some deep, dark, abandoned place within his soul, and it burst from his cracked and bleeding lips as the strangled voice of a stranger: "Eli, Eli, lema sabachthani?"

Then there came, like a swarm of rotten flies, some sour liquid that threatened to make him retch up all that was left inside, his very linings and organs. He moved his head away from it and swooned again.

The buzzing returned, and he tried to lift his head, but there was nothing left. The breath in his lungs carried his whisper—"It is finished"—and no more came in.

25

Retreat

I LEFT THE CRITIC and found myself once again in the studio, but this time, I was alone. I spun around, and it was as we had left it: the cloud, the oversized studio chair, and my own more normal-sized one. But the critic was gone.

I should have felt panic, for without the critic there was no guidance, not even the possibility of a return to the normalcy of existence—but instead, I appreciated the solitude and the chance to think. I knew, too, that was the reason for my solitude.

I had just witnessed a horrific murder. I had seen the baby as a man, shredded and broken, framed against the stormy skies amid the stench of a garbage heap. I had seen him, ragged and bloody from the injuries within and without, strain his mangled feet against the spike and the footrest to lift himself slightly enough to be able to take a breath.

I saw the same frailness, the same vulnerability to the savagery of the universe, that I had witnessed at his birth, but this time I saw him succumb.

Had I seen only a man, it would have been a horrid tragedy—but I still saw in him the all of Eternity, the potential for existence itself—and I saw him and all of that expire. And then I finally understood the sacrifice.

It was not, as I'd been taught, a man laying down his life in some way that purified my own. That made no sense, had no meaning. The gift was in the acceptance of life *and* death by one who did not need it, did not have to experience it. It was in the beginning and ending of an infinity, because through it I understood that my infinitesimal segment had meaning, that I was part of something that mattered and that already resounded, without beginning and without end, beyond existence itself, throughout Eternity.

He had offered me a drink, and I had sipped it.

26

The Promise

(THE CRITIC'S NARRATIVE)

I EMERGED FIRST, SHOCK draining all sensation from my head, a roaring replacing it. The Artist emerged next, a peaceful expression on his face, turned to me, and waited.

Finally, I spoke. "They treated you like an animal! They tore you to ribbons, nailed you to that contraption, and planted it in a garbage heap. How could you take that? Why didn't you just change them, change everything?"

"That was not my purpose. I am very proud to say that I stayed with it, that I didn't give up, even when I began to doubt my own sanity. I experienced what it meant to live as a finite being, and I experienced what it meant to have courage."

"Yes, I saw all that. But how could you watch yourself *die*?" I was shouting.

"That is the most difficult part of all this for me. You see, I had to experience death as they do. At that point, there was no connection between my eternal self and my finite self. I can see it through my earthly eyes, or I can see it through my Father's—through my eternal eyes. But unlike the rest of my life as Jesus, I cannot see it with a *unified* sense of self.

"As Jesus, at the moment of my death, every sense of who I am is about to cease to exist. Everything is about to end. I am alone in the universe.

"From my eternal perspective, however, I look at the death of Jesus as I see the death of every other creature in the world. I cannot identify with it.

"It's either one or the other. It's never both. Unless you experience it as yourself, you can't understand it."

"No, no, I can't understand it. But there was more to the story, wasn't there?" I asked.

"Oh, yes. Let's go back in and you can see what happens next." The Artist smiled and extended his arm in invitation.

When we again emerged from the cloud, I was smiling. "Well, I must say, that was a showstopper!"

The Artist laughed. "Yes, I suppose it was." He then grew serious. "But did you see how it changed them? For the first time in their lives—for the first time in human history—they saw a dead man bring himself back to life. Death could be defeated—and I had told them before that they, too, will one day overcome death.

"They had already seen me raise a dead man to life, my earthly friend Lazarus—but it was one thing to see that and another to see me overcome death myself. With that act, everything I had taught them suddenly took on a different meaning. There were a few who already believed I was God, or the Son of God—but even they weren't prepared for my resurrection."

The Artist smiled, shaking his head. "At that point, they were willing to go through anything, even death itself, just to tell others about me and to spread my message. And my message was *love*."

Suddenly, he threw open his arms, startling me, and I stepped back. "Do you see how it all changed? Before, I was trying to develop a relationship of love with my creations, but they kept trying to turn it into a system of rules and prestige. At the point I entered their world, even someone who *wanted* to find truth couldn't find it; their priests and religions had made it all too confusing. But now"—his eyes were gleaming—"now it has become about each individual person. All that matters is what each individual chooses to do."

"But even after your resurrection, what they call religion takes over and they do all kinds of horrible things in your name," I replied. "Is that also what you wanted?"

"Not at all, but that is part of their ability to choose. Just as always, those who love only themselves find a way to pervert love," answered the Artist. "But I gave them an ultimate answer. I told them, 'I am the way and the truth and the life.' Some took that to mean that only what they call 'Christianity' was valid, but they missed that all three of those paths were equal to me. They can pursue the Christian Way, following in the example I set; they can pursue the truth; and they can pursue a life in relationship with me. Any one of those will work and makes it possible for someone to enter Eternity who has never even heard of Jesus Christ.

"I built the desire for truth into their very souls. Some of them still choose to ignore it, becoming content with whatever they've already found. Others find a little truth and then stop, believing they have the whole package, and often even convince others who are gullible to accept that package as well.

"But those who never stop searching, those are who I want with me in Eternity."

I stood silent, bothered by something. "What is it?" asked the Artist.

"Most of them believe that you are going to judge their behavior, and that will determine whether or not they are with you in 'heaven.'"

"Yes," answered the Artist, "they have made it rather complicated. It's actually quite simple. What they call 'sin' is simply when they place their own desires above what they know to be my desire for them. It's always about love, that's all."

"But something else bothers me even more," I responded. "You have promised them a judgment day, and you have promised that all the dead will rise—but I don't see that anywhere in this work. Are you misleading them?"

"Not at all," laughed the Artist. "I just haven't finished the work yet. Once I do, what you see now will still be there, but there will be a new dimension to it. Quite frankly, I'm rather delighted with how surprised they will be by how it all happens!"

"What do you mean?" I asked.

"I told my followers when I was among them that they would not even taste death before they would see my kingdom come. Yet they all died; in fact, every single human dies, just as I told them when the humans first defied my will. You saw in the cloud that the time comes when humanity is simply finished, when the last human dies away." I nodded. "What they don't realize is that everything in their history has already happened and is still happening. They're blinded by their sense of time into thinking that the past is dead and the future has yet to occur, when in fact it's all right there.

"When I am fully satisfied with my work, I am simply going to bring those who love me into Eternity, right from the arc of their lives, across the entire breadth of *Existence*. They'll experience the higher dimensions at that point and come to me.

"Every single one of those self-chosen people will be brought into Eternity before they die, throughout all of time. They'll be able to go back and see themselves die, but they'll also be apart from it, already in Eternity. They'll have full access to the cloud itself. The scientists can explore the multiverse to their hearts' content, the historians can witness whatever they want to witness—they'll all be free to experience every aspect of both *Existence* and Eternity itself.

"The only limitation is that they will only experience Eternity through me. They'll know me as Jesus, and I will show them Eternity, and they will even join with me in creating my next work, just as the angels were involved in creating this one.

"But at this point, I am content with what I've created, and I am not ready to move on to another experience. This is my masterpiece, and I am not yet finished with it."

Emergence

IT HAPPENED AS DOES *the morning—he simply awakened and opened his eyes, but saw . . . everything. For a moment, he was bewildered, for there was simply too much to take in—but then, as if he were recovering from spinning too rapidly, his senses settled and he began to understand.*

For he was in a cloud, but it was a cloud of himself. In all directions he could see himself—as a baby suckling from his mother for the very first time, as a child catapulting himself over the low stone wall into his neighbor's field, as a young man feeling the touch of his beloved's fingers for the first time—and as the weak, dried-out husk that he had not yet become when he had wakened, riddled with cancers and fighting for every breath.

It was a life of love and mistakes, joy and pain, and it was his. He felt its every moment, and where there was shame, there was also understanding and the sense of honor in having turned out well. He knew he was loved, and he felt his Maker's approval and knew that the One for whom he had searched was right there behind him.

But he did not yet turn around. Instead, he seemed to stand up—and suddenly saw before him vistas of other lives, other stories, other landscapes—and even beyond those, other universes—and he felt—no, knew—that he could go to any of them with a single giant step.

But first, he turned around, not to a sight, but to a well of sound—a vast roaring voice that was also quiet and gentle, reminding him of the sensation of his ears at times in his life when they at last popped after descending from a great height—but this was a vastness of voice, the voice of his Maker, saying a word that took in everything he was, everything he knew, and gave it all to him as if giving him a life-saving breath.

And he breathed it out himself, and then suddenly before him was Eternity.

Q&A

WHY ARE YOU INTERVIEWING yourself?

I was constrained by the limitations of the narrative from explaining everything involved in this perspective on the Biblical description of creation. I also knew that there would inevitably be objections and even assumptions about my own personal beliefs. I therefore chose this format to address issues and ideas more thoroughly.

Besides, I had a lot of questions to ask myself, and I wanted to see the answers.

Do you really believe that there is a critic, that God has a studio, that existence is a cloud, etc.?

No. As noted in the preface and text, these are all literary devices—my choices for presenting ideas in a narrative format.

Do you believe that everything you had God say in this narrative is true?

No—but I believe they *could* be true, and that is the point of this narrative. My purpose was to engage the reader in thinking about God very differently than the traditional perspective. We who believe claim that God exists—but then we regard him as "spirit," like a ghost—and in fact, the Holy Spirit has even been called the "Holy Ghost." We are told that God is in heaven, seated on a throne, so we tend to imagine him as existing in some ethereal realm.

But even though we believe he exists, we don't tend to imagine him as *real*.

We also make the mistake of thinking of God as "existing," when everything that exists is his creation. God created existence itself; his place is in eternity. Why is this important? Because "existence" implies "nonexistence." Eternity has no beginning, no end—it is incompatible with the idea of existence.

So my purpose was to use a smattering of quantum theory as well as a perspective from *outside* existence and portray God's relationship with us as one between ourselves and a real entity with motivations and experiences.

So you believe that God is really an artist who created everything we know as a work of art?

Yes. This perspective is entirely consistent with the Bible and with the world as we—including scientists—know it. Ephesians 2:10 (NLT) tells us that we are God's "masterpiece." Proverbs 8:22–31 portrays God as a craftsman, with each of us among the "first of his works." In Matthew 13:10–11, Jesus explains that he tells stories to prepare his listeners for insight. In Exodus 35:30—36:1, God has an artistic vision for a tabernacle and appoints the human artists who will render it. And, of course, there is the story of creation itself in Genesis, as well as numerous exhortations throughout the rest of the Bible to worship, praise, or give thanks to God for the wonders of his creation.

Our standard ideas about God's purpose are circular reasoning. God created us to be in relationship with him. Why? Because God loves us. Usually, that's the end of speculation about God's general motive for our creation; beyond that point, we shrug and say that it is beyond us to understand God's thoughts.

But God wants us to know him, wants us to seek him out, wants us to grow in our understanding of him. The Bible itself is one demonstration of that fact; the discoveries by scientists of the intricacies of how things were created and how they work is yet another. We were made to be curious, and God has given us plenty to examine.

Perhaps new to my portrayal of God in this narrative is my emphasis upon his role as artist. I am proposing that the purpose of *all* art is to provide new perspectives on the world around us. This is why we value art that is fresh, unique, and original. Without this constant renewal from both art and our own artistic sensibilities, we would be as likely to stop and admire the beauty of a sunset as does a rabbit hopping through a meadow.

I extend this artistic purpose to God himself—and since art is always based in the context of the artist's own world, God's art would have to be about his own context—eternity—and the contrast between existence and nonexistence would be his artistic device for bringing a fresh perspective to the reality of eternity.

You have the Artist saying in chapter 26 that Christians often misinterpret the statement "I am the way and the truth and the life." Can you elaborate on this point?

Most interpretations seem to focus on the first two words and the fact that Jesus is saying them. But Jesus is saying that he is the way, he is the truth, and he is the life—$a = b$, $a = c$, and $a = d$—which also means that $a = b = c = d$, and $d = c = b = a$. He is saying that those who follow him will know the Father, as will those who follow the Way—the principles he is teaching everyone (since Christianity does not yet exist)—those who search for the truth, and those who live their lives according to the Father's will.

If one "follows the Way"—attempts to live by the principles of Christianity as described by Christ himself—that person will "know the Father." However, the person who seeks the truth—who goes beyond teachings and continues to question and learn—will also know the Father. This includes anyone before or after Christ and those of other faiths; however, it does not include those who are complacent with what they know already (including Christians). Finally, it includes those who are spiritual and look to Christ for guidance, or who follow God's will for them. It is common to add "without question" to that last phrase, but Christ himself questioned God's will even while he accepted it in the Garden of Gethsemane. We are questioning creatures; we were made to question, and we are therefore meant to question.

This makes much more sense than trying to construe things so that a religious movement that starts in the midst of human history and is unavailable to at least half of the world is the only way anyone can ever be saved. I still subscribe to the belief that Christianity is the closest to the truth—but even so, Christians cannot be complacent with their faith and knowledge. They must continue to search for truth.

The reason I wrote this narrative is that I wanted to find a truth beyond what is contained within the Bible. The Bible is a guide to understanding God; it does not contain everything there is to know about God. For the rest, we have access to his creation through science, art, and of course, our own personal experiences and revelations.

You include a depiction of the crucifixion but not the resurrection. Why?

This narrative tries to portray the story from God's perspective. Given his eternal nature, his most momentous experience is his own death, his own ending. It is also the moment when he is apparently cut off from eternity itself. I entitled it "Exegesis" because it is the moment of clarity, explanation, and understanding from *both* our perspective and his. The resurrection is an incredible event to humans, but to God, it was simply the return to his natural state—probably more a moment of relief than revelation.

Christianity claims the resurrection to be the ultimate moment and celebrates it through Easter—and yet the symbol of Christianity is the cross. The fact that death could be beaten, that Eternity is ultimately won for all of us, is the message of Easter—but somehow, we Christians understand that the sacrifice of Christ must be our constant reminder. The significance of the resurrection is easy for us mortals to grasp—yet I have never heard an explanation for the crucifixion that felt visceral. "He died for our sins" or "He died that we might live" are abstract ideas that do not seem to resonate throughout the minutes of each day, but I can gaze upon a sunset and feel in the sight of it my own mortality as well as my hope for eternity.

I hope that this entire book gives impact to my depiction of the crucifixion. Every time I read it, I am overwhelmed by the enormity of the willingness of an eternal deity to die while cut off from every sense of eternity. Asking God why he, Jesus, has been forsaken is a staggering moment when one considers it in the context of the rest of this book.

In your own preface, and in the use of the critic character, you suggest that God has an audience beyond humans and the angels. The implications are that God is not a unique entity. Do you believe this to be true?

This is where I know I am stepping off a cliff. I should emphasize that I am quite willing to be found wrong on this issue as well as all the other conclusions to which I have come in this narrative.

The critic, of course, is simply a character, a literary device. I am not suggesting at all that there is such an entity.

There is, however, some Biblical foundation to the idea that God is not alone. While God's use of the words "we" and "us" to refer to himself throughout Genesis—as in Genesis 1:26 where he also refers to making humans in "our own image"—is usually explained to be the "royal we," it is not used that way elsewhere in the Bible. Psalm 82:1 states that "God presides in the great assembly; he gives judgment among the 'gods.'" There are similar references in Psalms 86 and 89. These are usually interpreted to refer to representatives of God on earth, such as judges. But that interpretation is certainly elevating such human representatives to a level not portrayed anywhere else in the Bible. Quite frankly, believing that humans could serve in a "great assembly" over which God himself simply "presides" seems to me to be hubris.

Throughout the Bible, we are exhorted to worship no other gods but God himself. However, nowhere in the Bible does it explicitly tell us that there *are* no other gods. We usually interpret the first commandment to refer to the false gods that humans tend to create when left to their own devices. But could this also have been a warning to stay away from other gods who may step into the picture from time to time?

I am not sure about that at all—but I *am* sure that since God is my Creator, I have no business with other gods regardless of who they are or where they come from. I regard the character of the critic and the references to other "denizens of Eternity" to be only literary devices.

However, God *is* in a context of his own (I am studiously trying to avoid words like "being" and "exist" when referring to him), and nothing in our own reality suggests that anything can be only one of a kind. I also find it rather dissatisfying to think that God created us as both art and audience. To me, it is not unreasonable to assume that where there is an artist, there is an audience.

Still, all the concepts in this book could be considered without any dependence upon or reference to other entities.

You also refer to earlier creations and creations yet to come.

I find it fascinating that angels are treated only as, at best, tangential characters in the Bible. The "war in heaven" referred to in Revelation 12:7 does seem to indicate another story outside of our own. Randy Alcorn, who has focused his ministry and teachings on what we know of heaven, has suggested that angels exist only in direct relationship to God and lack both the communal instinct and the wider range of human emotions. Nevertheless, the war in heaven establishes that angels also possess freedom of choice. Given my notion of sequence in eternity as the equivalent of time, the angels' story is apparently already resolved by the start of the Bible, since the serpent is at that point working against what God has commanded—thus indicating a preexisting enmity.

Beyond even the angels' story, there is also the reference to us as God's "masterpiece." A masterpiece implies workmanship and craft—and it also implies lesser prior achievements. This also supports the concept of sequence applying to God and, thus, eternity.

Alcorn argues that there are adventures yet to come once judgment day is over and we are sharing in God's rule. And, of course, for an eternal artist, there would never be an end to the production of art. If we will "reign with him" (2 Timothy 2:12), then we will have responsibilities and power within what can only be further experiences.

You refer to "sequence" as the equivalent of time in eternity. Where do you get that idea?

The character of God in the Bible develops from beginning to end. I have always found this intriguing, given that God is also both eternal and unchanging. From Genesis, where God acts primarily as a friend in the garden to Adam and Eve; to the rest of the Old Testament, where he is judgmental, demanding, intercessional, and wrathful; to the New Testament, where he becomes our loving Father, there are considerable changes. While it is usually argued that these are simply different facets of his character being exposed at different points, I have been especially intrigued by the argument on Mount Sinai between Moses and God, in which God wants to kill all the people, and then *changes his mind* in response to Moses' appeal (Exodus 32:11–14). In Genesis 6:7, God actually regrets a past action. If God is unchanging, then how can one reconcile the God who says during creation that "it is good" with the God who then says in chapter 6, "I regret that I have made them"?

What I am proposing is that, even in eternity, there is a "before" and "after." However, since God is unchanging, once something happens he is aware of it throughout eternity; in other words, he grows in *experience*. Note that even creation is an act, with a before and after; if God's creation had always existed, why would there be the need for the act of creation described in the Bible?

Your description of the Artist creating existence uses a particle of eternity as the source of all matter and energy. Is this just a mystical way of avoiding the scientific issues?

Actually, I am intrigued by how well this idea satisfies both Biblical and scientific themes. When negative and positive matter come together, they annihilate each other (although matter and energy are still conserved)—just as a negative number and its positive number, when added together, become zero. We have always regarded zero as the absence of existence. But since, in my narrative, existence is a contained work of art in the context of eternity, one could extend my description of the Artist's creation as implying that zero is representative of eternity. Existence is bound by issues of physics, dependent upon energy, matter, and physical laws. Eternity does not have any definitive limitations whatsoever. To use it as a source point for polarities is the same as equating it to what we in our world refer to as "nothing."

Besides, according to physicists who subscribe to a finite universe, beyond where the universe ends is *really* nothing—not even dark energy. To me, this implies that nothing is the default state.

We could therefore consider the possibility that nothing, or zero, has the qualities of eternity. It is important to note that eternity is not equivalent to "forever" or "infinity." Both of those terms can be defined as having a starting or focal point; eternity does not. Likewise, "heaven" is an earlier creation—not eternity—and "paradise" seems to refer specifically to the redeemed form of the world or universe we already know (whatever one perceives as "perfect" would exist among probabilities and can thus be observed).

A human being in eternity would probably be incapable of truly experiencing eternity. After all, a human being is made of definitive properties; eternity is not. Or, at least, eternity is not made of properties defined by our own matter- and energy-related laws. However, the Bible promises us that we will experience eternity through the eternal person of the divine Jesus. Given our physical constraints, that actually makes sense.

Do I really believe all this? No, I just find the idea intriguing. If one considers the idea of eternity seriously, what we know of it would fall completely outside the boundaries of anything we know. When you remove all physical properties from a phenomenon, you end up with, well, zero. And our universe, or even the multiverse—indeed, existence itself—is a phenomenon.

You also refer to a "multiverse" and other concepts from quantum theory. How accurate are these references?
I have used some of the most widely accepted concepts from quantum theory but only referred to them with the broadest of

strokes. I do believe that quantum physicists are drawing closer to some of the basics of God's own craftsmanship, and I find their discoveries very exciting. For me, the turning point was discovering that the act of observation changes the phenomenon, and that both energy and matter are represented by wave functions representing the probability that such particles exist at any point in time or space. However, the actual observation of the particle collapses the wave function and renders the particle in a fixed three- or four-dimensional position. In *Parallel Worlds*, Michio Kaku suggests that anything that can be imagined has a probability factor for it to actually occur, and that if we could control outcomes to increase the probabilities of occurrences, anything would literally be possible—similar to the "improbability drive" in Douglas Adams's *The Hitchhiker's Guide to the Galaxy*.

If there is a God, then he already controls those probabilities. Thus, the miracles of the Old Testament as well as the miracles of Jesus are all simply the result of changing the probability of certain outcomes.

The multiverse concept from quantum theory also helped me resolve several traditional issues concerning science and theology. Quantum physicists have already theorized that there are multiple universes and have even begun attempts to detect them indirectly. Some use the concept of the multiverse to again eliminate the need for a deity by theorizing that the fact of our existence is simply the outcome of the law of averages: given the seemingly infinite number of possible universes with different physical laws, there would be one in which everything comes together in optimal combination to support the development of life.

As noted in the narrative in the example of the statue, I used this approach to provide a rationale for the focus on humans within the context of the creation of everything, of existence itself: what came before the creation of humankind (and what comes after) is but the stuff of the statue's interior—it provides the support for the actual featured artwork, the surfaces of the statue. Likewise, God's focus is on the part of our universe concerned with humans.

I realize this comes perilously close to the proposal by some anti-evolutionists that fossils were created to be fossils and were never actually creatures in the past. That is not what I am suggesting. I *am* suggesting that other universes and everything that has happened and will happen from the singularity (the possible initial state of our universe) to the Big Bang to the appearance of humankind and even to the end of everything after the end of humanity do in fact occur—but all of that is simply "statue stuffing."

So our universe is the real universe? Isn't that bordering on a conceit similar to other humanly egocentric ideas such as the pre-Galilean concept of the Earth being the center of the universe?

To be honest, what I really believe was too complex to render in the narrative. I will attempt to explain it here, though.

The electron forms a shell or cloud around the nucleus of the atom because there are levels of probability for that electron at every point in its orbit around the nucleus. But if you trap that electron at a particular point in space-time so that you can identify its actual position, that shell collapses and you are left with only that electron in that position. A particular reality has now been defined. Release the electron, and probabilities begin again, but now they emanate in degree from the position at which the electron was once defined.

What was hardest for me to fathom was the revelation in quantum mechanics that probability is a wave function that is inherently part of our universe's physical structure. I refer readers to the books by Michio Kaku for clearer explanations of this astounding idea. Probability shapes not only our universe but others as well.

Many prominent scientists argue that time itself is not real. I strongly recommend Lee Smolin's provocative book *Time Reborn: From the Crisis in Physics to the Future of the Universe.* Smolin makes a convincing argument for the necessity of time even within quantum physics.

Based on what I have read in Kaku's and others' quantum physics books for the layman, string theory physicists seem to define universes according to their physical laws. Change the strength of one of the nuclear forces and you get an entirely different universe, for example.

But they also refer to universes differing from ours only by the differences generated by changes at the subatomic level. These universes vary in *probability*. If one were to go back to the birth of the multiverse, then a very fine difference in the nuclear forces could have generated universes with different physical laws—but that could have been the difference between our universe having a 99.999+ percent probability of having the nuclear forces we have, and another universe having a 99.998+ percent probability of having slightly different nuclear forces.

Lee Smolin argues in *Time Reborn* that the idea of every probability existing in separate universes renders the idea of science itself (and therefore the objective search for truth) as unsustainable, since every possibility and any experimental outcome is real somewhere. He is also the one who introduced me to the idea of the forward arrow of time leading to greater improbabilities. While he may not appreciate how I've applied them, his arguments, as well as his explanation of qualia, led me to the many conjunctions of the concepts of our individual experiences of time progression, the principle of observation defining reality, and the notion of spirituality as our individual defining experiences, physically expressed by our ability to choose from among probabilities—my own definition of life itself.

Are you sure about that?

No. It is not my intention to portray myself as an expert in quantum physics. I am simply an interested layman who understands little if any of the mathematics involved. But the quantum theories and discoveries are beginning to give us the capability of imagining God in a more real and defined context—which was the purpose of this narrative.

Afterword

Does God exist? In this book I have been toying with a branch of science—quantum physics—that has led many scientists to believe in God and, at the same time, led others to even greater confidence that reality can be explained without the need for a creator.

However, one of humanity's greatest mistakes in its thinking is to anthropomorphize or assume that what we know as our own reality is, by necessity, the universal standard. Quantum physicists are already beginning to realize, however, that there could be universes out there that have very different physical laws than our own. If anything is possible in physics, then so is something approximating God in another universe, even if our own, as some insist on arguing, does not need a God. I remain surprised that no one appears to have explicitly stated this scientifically compatible conclusion.

But that is simply circular reasoning. Does God as commonly portrayed in the religions really exist?

The God of the Bible is largely anthropomorphized—which makes sense because we would otherwise be unable to understand what the Bible wants us to know about him. However, as noted before, anthropomorphosis is usually a mistake.

The question in physics is whether reality as we understand it requires an intelligent designer. For a moment, consider what those two words actually mean.

Consider the word "designer." Many quantum physicists, such as the late Stephen Hawking, believe that our universe can be explained without reliance upon a creator. Indeed, in his *A Briefer*

History of Time, Hawking makes the argument that since particles without a point of beginning exist in the subatomic world, one can construct a circular causation pattern that does not require a creator because there is no starting point.

However, the reason the question keeps arising is because physics clearly portrays patterns or design. Those convinced that a creator is involved argue that a design always signifies a designer. That is actually a truth: even if everything is the product of self-contained forces, those forces are in fact the designer.

The real question, then, focuses on the first word: Is the designer *intelligent*?

An intelligent designer would be a being with a purpose for creating reality—even if that purpose is nothing more than a form of doodling. However, once we start adding the words "being" and "purpose," we have once again begun to anthropomorphize.

The fact is that we exist in a reality of expressed purpose—even if that expression is only the result of an internally contained design. We have cause, effect, function and role in every element we discover. What we discover around us is either the fulfillment of purpose or the process that involves elements in fulfilling that purpose: the eye has a purpose, photosynthesis has a purpose, and the woman walking down the street has a purpose. Our universe is a system of elements that fulfill purposes. Things like an appendix are troublesome because they no longer have a perceivable purpose.

As scientists try to derive through mathematics and observation a universal theory for everything, they are simply trying to discover that original engine, the source for our existence. In doing so, they are pursuing the same question that every theologian and philosopher also pursue: Why?

However, what is being overlooked is that intelligence does not have to reside in an organic brain. If we do, indeed, find that formula for everything, or discover the complete details of the pattern that Hawking believes to exist, then we will be looking at a designer of sorts.

Do we then claim that source not to be intelligent simply because it is not organic or because it cannot be defined as a being? Consider our primary exploratory tool, mathematics. If SETI (Search for Extraterrestrial Intelligence) were to receive a message from space expressing mathematical relationships and formulae, we would believe we had contacted an alien intelligence.

But that has already happened. We have been discovering a message of mathematical relationships since we first began to calculate. Mathematics itself has been a code that has led us to discover realities both within and beyond our ability to observe.

And mathematics is not a human creation. Its principles are a discovery of something that already exists. Did the universe result from mathematics, or did mathematics result from the universe? If the very first process in the Big Bang followed mathematical principles, then mathematics begets the universe.

And our universe is, in fact, an expression of mathematical relationships.

Quite simply, mathematics itself could be a designer. If we at last discover the unified formula from which all mathematical relationships and physical laws could be derived, then that formula as a function could be viewed as the designer of our universe.

I am not proposing that mathematics really is the architect of our existence; I am using it as an example to expand the possibilities for a designer beyond an anthropomorphic concept. If something is brought into existence—even through a cyclical big bang process—then it must be contained within a larger context. At that point, such words as "intelligent" and "being"—both as a noun and as a state—become useless.

If we discard our requirement that God must be a being, then we are no longer asking if there is a force beyond our existence that somehow produced it. Instead, we are left with a question as complex as the pattern of existence itself: What is the context of the source of the expressed purpose in which we exist, and does that source pursue purposes beyond our existence?

That is a question about the nature, not the existence, of God—and it encompasses the domain of both theology and science. That question, however, is supplemental to a simple question with a simple answer.

Does God exist?

Yes.

Acknowledgments

I AM GRATEFUL TO many people who played a role in helping me to write this book. First, I want to thank my wife Debbie for putting up with me sharing my latest ideas and supporting my writing vacations away from home so that I could spend several days simply focusing on the book. Likewise, I owe my son Michael gratitude for trying to understand my ideas while he was still growing up.

I also want to thank my daughter. Erica is the one who found Wipf and Stock Publishers, and she served as the line editor for *The Creator's Craft*. She also suggested Alex Paterson as the copy editor. I am grateful to both of them for their diligence, insights and support.

Luke Davis, my son-in-law, went beyond expectations in creating a variety of illustration options for the images used in the narrative. He is an incredible artist, and I deeply appreciate his efforts.

I was guided in my Christian journey by the following: Charlie McMahan, senior pastor for SouthBrook Christian Church; Larry Schwiekart, fellow SouthBrook member and University of Dayton colleague; my good friend Nick Cardilino; and my dear friend and spiritual mentor, Vaughn Welches.

While my education in quantum physics was mostly guided by my reading, I owe a debt of gratitude to Daniel Whiteson of the podcast *Daniel and Jorge Explain the Universe*. Daniel never read my book, nor did I share any of its original concepts with him, but he has been extraordinarily patient and supportive in replying to my email questions and ideas. Likewise, I want to thank my friend

Jim Chalker, physics teacher, who did read an earlier version of this book and provided valuable feedback.

Finally, I want to thank Wipf and Stock for the publication of *The Creator's Craft* and for their support in preparing it for printing.

Bibliography

Alcorn, Randy. *Heaven.* Wheaton, IL: Tyndale House, 2004.

——. *In Light of Eternity: Perspectives on Heaven.* Colorado Springs: WaterBrook, 1999.

——. *Money, Possessions & Eternity.* Wheaton, IL: Tyndale House, 2003.

Al-Khalili, Jim. *Quantum: A Guide for the Perplexed.* London: Weidenfeld & Nicolson, 2003.

Aslan, Reza. *Zealot: The Life and Times of Jesus of Nazareth.* New York: Random House, 2013.

Baggott, Jim. *Farewell to Reality: How Modern Physics Has Betrayed the Search for Scientific Truth.* New York: Pegasus Books, 2013.

——. *Quantum Space: Loop Quantum Gravity and the Search for the Structure of Space, Time, and the Universe.* Oxford: Oxford University Press, 2019.

Bryson, Bill. *A Short History of Nearly Everything.* Read by Richard Matthews. New York: Books on Tape, 2003. CD, 18 hr.

Carroll, Sean. *The Big Picture: On the Origins of Life, Meaning, and the Universe Itself.* New York: Dutton, 2016.

——. *From Eternity to Here: The Quest for the Ultimate Theory of Time.* New York: Dutton, 2010.

——. *The Particle at the End of the Universe: How the Hunt for the Higgs Boson Leads Us to the Edge of a New World.* New York: Dutton, 2012.

——. *Something Deeply Hidden: Quantum Worlds and the Emergence of Spacetime.* New York: Dutton, 2019.

Ehrman, Bart. D. *Jesus, Interrupted: Revealing the Hidden Contradictions in the Bible (and Why We Don't Know about Them).* New York: HarperOne, 2009.

Eldredge, John. *Epic: The Story God Is Telling.* Nashville: Thomas Nelson, 2004.

——. *Wild at Heart: Discovering the Secret of a Man's Soul.* Nashville: Thomas Nelson, 2001.

Goldberg, Dave. *The Universe in the Rearview Mirror: How Hidden Symmetries Shape Reality.* New York: Dutton, 2013.

Greene, Brian. *The Elegant Universe: Superstrings, Hidden Dimensions, and the Quest for the Ultimate Theory.* Read by Erik Davies. New York: Random House Audio, 2008. eAudiobook, 15 hr., 36 min.

———. *The Hidden Reality: Parallel Universes and the Deep Laws of the Cosmos.* Read by the author. New York: Random House Audio, 2011. Audio CD, 14 hr.

———. *Until the End of Time: Mind, Matter, and Our Search for Meaning in an Evolving Universe.* New York: Alfred A. Knopf, 2020.

Hawking, Stephen. *A Brief History of Time: From the Big Bang to Black Holes.* New York: Bantam Books, 1988.

Hawking, Stephen, and Leonard Mlodinow. *A Briefer History of Time.* New York: Bantam Books, 2005.

Kaku, Michio. *Einstein's Cosmos: How Albert Einstein's Vision Transformed Our Understanding of Space and Time.* Read by Ray Porter. N.p.: Audible Studios, 2013. eAudiobook, 6 hr., 30 min.

———. *Parallel Worlds: A Journey through Creation, Higher Dimensions, and the Future of the Cosmos.* New York: Doubleday, 2005.

———. *Physics of the Future: How Science Will Shape Human Destiny and Our Daily Lives by the Year 2100.* Read by Feodor Chin. New York: Random House Audio, 2011. Audio CD, 16 hr.

———. *Physics of the Impossible: A Scientific Exploration into the World of Phasers, Force Fields, Teleportation, and Time Travel.* New York: Doubleday, 2008.

Kumar, Manjit. *Quantum: Einstein, Bohr, and the Great Debate about the Nature of Reality.* New York: W. W. Norton, 2008.

Lane, Nick. *The Vital Question: Energy, Evolution, and the Origins of Complex Life.* New York: W. W. Norton, 2015.

McLaren, Brian. D. *A New Kind of Christian: A Tale of Two Friends on a Spiritual Journey.* San Francisco: Jossey-Bass, 2001.

Muller, Richard. A. *Now: The Physics of Time.* Read by Christopher Grove. New York: Random House Audio, 2016. eAudiobook, 10 hr., 3 min.

Panek, Richard. *The 4% Universe: Dark Matter, Dark Energy, and the Race to Discover the Rest of Reality.* Read by Ray Porter. Ashland, OR: Blackstone Audio, 2011. eAudiobook, 10 hr., 7 min.

Rovelli, Carlo. *The Order of Time.* New York: Riverhead Books, 2018.

———. *Reality Is Not What It Seems: The Journey to Quantum Gravity.* Read by Roy McMillan. New York: Penguin Audio, 2017. eAudiobook, 6 hr. 10 min.

Schilling, Govert. *Ripples in Spacetime: Einstein, Gravitational Waves, and the Future of Astronomy.* Cambridge, MA: Belknap Press of Harvard University Press, 2017.

Smolin, Lee. *Time Reborn: From the Crisis in Physics to the Future of the Universe.* Boston: Houghton Mifflin Harcourt, 2013.

———. *The Trouble with Physics: The Rise of String Theory, The Fall of a Science, and What Comes Next.* Read by Walter Dixon. N.p.: Audible Studios, 2010. eAudiobook, 14 hr. 49 min.

Whiteson, Daniel, and Jorge Cham. *Daniel and Jorge Explain the Universe.* iHeartMedia, 2018. Podcast, MP3 audio. https://www.iheart.com/podcast/1119-daniel-and-jorge-explain-225021599/.

Witherington, Ben. "Bart Interrupted—A detailed Analysis of 'Jesus Interrupted.'" Parts 1–4 and coda. *Ben Witherington* (blog), April 7–20, 2009. http://benwitherington.blogspot.com/.

———. *The Gospel Code: Novel Claims About Jesus, Mary Magdalene, and Da Vinci.* Read by Grover Gardner. Escondido, CA: christianaudio, 2009. eAudiobook, 5 hr., 57 min.